Duffle Bag Cartel 6

Ghost

Lock Down Publications and Ca$h
Presents
Duffle Bag Cartel 6
A Novel by *Ghost*

Ghost

Lock Down Publications
P.O. Box 944
Stockbridge, Ga 30281

Visit our website @
www.lockdownpublications.com

Copyright 2021 by Ghost
Duffle Bag Cartel 6

Lock Down Publications
Like our page on Facebook: Lock Down Publications
@
www.facebook.com/lockdownpublications.ldp

Book interior design by: **Shawn Walker**

4

Stay Connected with Us!

Text **LOCKDOWN** to 22828 to stay up-to-date with new releases, sneak peaks, contests and more…
Thank you.

Submission Guideline.

Submit the first three chapters of your completed manuscript to ldpsubmissions@gmail.com, subject line: Your book's title. The manuscript must be in a .doc file and sent as an attachment. Document should be in Times New Roman, double spaced and in size 12 font. Also, provide your synopsis and full contact information. If sending multiple submissions, they must each be in a separate email.

Have a story but no way to send it electronically? You can still submit to LDP/Ca$h Presents. Send in the first three chapters, written or typed, of your completed manuscript to:

LDP: Submissions Dept
P.O. Box 944
Stockbridge, Ga 30281

DO NOT send original manuscript. Must be a duplicate.

Provide your synopsis and a cover letter containing your full contact information.

Thanks for considering LDP and Ca$h Presents.

Dedications

This book is dedicated to the slums of Memphis, Tennessee, and the Stevens family as a whole. Y'all know how we get down.

Ghost

Chapter 1

"Ahhhhhhhhhhh! Ahhhhhhhh! What the fuck is wrong with you? Ahhhhhhhhhh!" Gunnah hollered before Skyy smacked the tape back over his mouth. Blood poured out of his missing cheek like an overflowing volcano.

Rondo held his cheek out for him to see it dangling from the vice grips. "See dis shit here, mane? What you gon' do?"

Gunnah stomped his feet on the ground as hard as he could. Tears ran down his face and mixed with the blood that was already there. He shook his head and bucked his eyes wide open.

"Betta play ball den, nigga." Skyy ripped the tape from his mouth.

Gunnah struggled to catch his breath. "Look, mane, I ain't giving y'all all of my shit. I'll give up half. I can't give up all because it doesn't belong to me. It ain't my money."

"Yeah, dis nigga wanna play games. Slap dat shit back over his mouth, mane," Rondo ordered.

Skyy did just that. "I can tell he finna cave. Claw him up again," she said, acting like the scene going on in front of her wasn't freaking her out as much as it was.

Rondo clamped the vice grips on to the tip of Gunnah's nose and tightened the claws. Once they were tightened, he began to pull with all of his might. Gunnah went crazy as he felt the skin break on both sides of his nose. He heard the flesh tearing and he fainted. When Skyy slapped him awake again, Rondo was standing in front of him holding the tip of his nose with plasma leaking from it.

"Let's see what he got to say now." Skyy pulled the tape from his face, and in the midst of doing so, wound up with blood all over her wrist and knuckles.

"Okay, man, okay. Fuck dis shit, but I'm telling you right now dat you don't understand. All da money dat you 'bout to take from me doesn't belong to me. It belongs to Jimmy Bands. Dis all his shit. Once he find out what y'all done did, he gon' kill yo' ass, Rondo, and yo' punk ass too, Skyy."

Rondo was thrown off. "Jimmy Bands? Nigga, you a ma'fuckin' lie. Jimmy don't fuck wit' Sniper Gang. That nigga Duffle Bag all day and until the world blow. Bitch, you lying."

"Call him den. Call that nigga and tell him what you doing to me and you're about to find out real fast. I bet you he tells you to leave me be. If he doesn't, you can smoke me right here and right now." Gunnah said this with his face dripping large amounts of blood.

"You know what? I'm fin' too." He pulled out his cell phone, ready to dial.

Skyy saw an abundance of cash flying out the window and had to stop the fiasco before it got started. Even if Gunnah was telling the truth, they were in too deep. She didn't give a fuck if the money belonged to Jimmy Bands or not. She wanted it. She grabbed Rondo's wrist. "Wait, baby, fuck calling Jimmy. He doesn't even like discussing bidness over da phone like dat. If all of this money is his, we can just give it to him later, but for now, let's finish the mission. Ain't yo' crew starving?"

Rondo looked around at his crew of hungry, starving, damn near broke teens. Most of them were from low-income housing, and the others were homeless. They needed this score, and he had to make it happen. If the money belonged to Jimmy Bands, he could always hit him with it later after asking for a percentage for his homies. "Yeah, you right. Look, Gunnah, the next thang I'ma do is rip yo' eyelids off. Give me the combination and direct me to the safes, or it's a wrap. What you gon' do?"

Gunnah closed his eyes. "I'll take you all over the house and give you what you want. Fuck Jimmy's money, dis shit ain't worth me dying over."

Skyy smiled. "Good answer."

***

It took twenty minutes for Rondo and his crew to locate and empty out every single vault inside of the safe house. By the time they were finished, they had come up on 1.5 million dollars in cash, twenty kilos of heroin, and fifteen of coke. Rondo loaded up his whips with the spoils and came back to the basement. "Looks like you were a good sport. Dat shit was in yo' best interest."

Skyy came down the steps and stood beside Rondo. "What we gon' do wit' his bitch ass now, baby?"

Rondo pulled his .45 out of the small of his back and cocked it. "It ain't what we 'bout to do, but what you 'bout to do." He looked over at her. "Dat nigga been beating on you since day one. Fucking you over just cause he paying a few of yo' bills. Dat's punk shit. Seems to me dat da best option is fo' you to take him out the game like he was just getting ready to do you. What you thank?"

Skyy became nervous. "I ain't never killed nobody before. I'm scared."

Rondo grabbed her and made her stand in front of him. "Bitch, wrap yo' hands around dis pole and let me guide yo' simple ass."

"Okay." Skyy did as she was told. She wrapped her hand around the gun and closed her eyes expecting a blast. When none came, she opened them.

Gunnah fought against his binds in his chair. Blood ran from his face and nose. He felt weak. He imagined what the bullet was going to feel like entering his body, and he started to shake. He was afraid of death.

Rondo guided the gun until it was pointed right at Gunnah's face. "Awright, shawty, thank 'bout all dem times dis nigga beat you or forced himself on you. Thank 'bout all dem times you hated yo'self after he climbed from yo' body. Den thank 'bout if he would have killed you just a li'l while ago."

Skyy frowned. Her heart began to beat harder and harder. "I hate you, Gunnah! I hate yo' stinking guts."

"Yeah, baby, hate dat nigga." Rondo ripped the tape from Gunnah's mouth. "Nigga, beg for yo' life. Maybe we'll save you."

"Please don't kill me. Please. I'm sorry, Skyy. I swear I'll never beat you again. I apologize, please."

"Yuck, nigga." Rondo slapped the duct tape back over his mouth. "Awright, you heard him beg. Now it's time to finish this nigga. Let's get it." Rondo placed his hands on top of hers, took her finger, and pulled the trigger, sending a bullet into Gunnah's Adam's apple.

Gunnah's head jerked backward and snapped his neck. He was dead as soon as the impact happened. The room splashed red at first, and then faded to black.

"Shoot that nigga again, baby," Rondo urged. He removed his finger this time

Skyy pulled the trigger again and again and again with her eyes closed. When she opened them, Gunnah was slumped over with his brains hanging out of his face like spaghetti. She sighed and jumped back.

Rondo mugged Gunnah's corpse. "Rest in blood, nigga."

That night, Jimmy Bands was still out of town on business. Rondo took it upon himself to send his loyal killas all around Orange Mound, door to door, knocking off loose members of the Sniper Gang. Before the night was concluded, thirty-one

Sniper Gang members had been killed, and over fifty had fled the hood with their lives intact for the moment.

***

When Jimmy Bands found out about the death of Gunnah, and how he had been stripped, he went ballistic. He grabbed May Baby and Rondo and rushed over to where Gunnah's body was. It had been kept in the same position, and everything. It had been found by two of Jimmy Bands' security team that rolled through to collect the funds that Gunnah had accrued for the week. When they got there, they'd found Gunnah stretched out and the house ransacked. Instead of contacting the local authorities, they hit up Jimmy and waited until he flew in from Port Au Prince, Haiti before they made another move.

Rondo played the situation close to his chest. He wanted to see what was really going on before he made his next move. He strolled about the house as if he had never been there before, shadowing Jimmy Bands.

Jimmy Bands squatted down in front of Gunnah's body and shook his head. "Fuck! Ain't dis 'bout a bitch?"

Rondo shook his head as he stood behind Jimmy Bands. "I don't understand, Blood. Why the fuck we care if dis nigga got slumped or not? He was just talking dat dumb shit a few weeks back."

Jimmy sighed. "Yeah, but I went over his head and got shit situated. All of dis money was mine. We had conquered the Sniper Game by a simple phone call. The Mound belonged to me, and it wasn't nothing dat Phoenix could do 'bout it. Fuck. The niggas took my whole stash. Dat nigga Phoenix finna come at my head. What am I gon' do?"

MayBaby came over and rubbed his shoulders. "We'll figure it out, baby. We always do. I wouldn't even worry 'bout it."

Jimmy Bands lowered his head again. "I gotta find out who did this shit, and I gotta whack they ass after I get my shit back. Ain't no way I can rebound from dis shit right hurr, mane. Only way I can is if I get my shit back. Fuck!" He punched his hand as hard as he could.

"Yeah, mane, well, you already know I'm wit' you. Just let me know what you wanna do, and we gon' get to it. Ride or die my nigga." Rondo pulled his nose and sniffed hard.

Jimmy Bands nodded and stood up. He faced Rondo and placed his hands on his shoulders. "Say mane, you help me find out who did dis and I got ten G's for you, li'l dawg. Hit the streets and bring me back that definite, and it's yours. What you say?"

"Ten G's? All of dat for me?" Rondo laughed. "Yeah, awright, nigga, dat sound like a bet." Rondo removed Jimmy Bands' hands off of his shoulders. "Before I go though, I need to know one thang."

"Damn, nigga, time is money. Fuck you wanna know?" Jimmy Bands muttered, irritated.

Rondo laughed a killer's laugh. "Dat nigga Phoenix was yo' big homie, right?

"Yeah, of course he was," Jimmy assured him.

"And he was feeding you and yo' family, and all of dat shit, right?" Rondo asked.

"Yeah, dat's a good nigga." Jimmy Bands had to admit.

"And you mean to tell me dat you lost all of his money, and all of yours too?" Rondo stepped back a tad.

"What, man? Hell nawl. I still got five million of my own money put up. I ain't dat stupid. Dat nigga shit just fucked off.

That's crazy though." Jimmy thought about his next move, and knew it had to be his best one.

"Yeah, it is crazy, 'cause I gotta have all of dat, my nigga."

Rondo upped two F&Ns and placed them to Jimmy Bands' face. His young armed goons came from all over the house and filled the living room, laying May Baby on her back with their guns aimed at her and Jimmy Bands.

"Nigga, I want all of dat bread, and everythang you got left. When I'm done wit' you, I'm stripping Phoenix too and smoking you niggas. There is a new day in Orange Mound, and there is a new leader of this here Cartel, and his mutha-fuckin' name is Rondo."

Ghost

Chapter 2

"And once again our top story today is that there are thirty-four confirmed cases of Coronavirus at the White House, including the President of the United States. Sources close to the White House say that the President's staff has been deeply affected by the virus, and many are very sick. Those that have come back with positive tests but are showing no symptoms are made to quarantine for the recommended fourteen days. When asked if those that are affected will be able to carry out their duties, the White House Correspondent declined to comment. In other news——"

Natalia took the remote from Taurus's hand and cut off the television. She stood in front of the screen with a smile on her face. "Well, Daddy, are you proud of me?" She knelt in front of him while he sat on the couch.

"What did you do, baby?" He looked down at her and placed his right hand on the side of her beautiful face.

"I did the opposite of what they wanted you to do. They wanted you to infect our people: the disenfranchised, the poor, and the defenseless. Well, I flipped the script and gave them a taste of their own medicine, and it didn't even cost me that much." She laughed. "You would be surprised at how much pull your baby girl really has when it comes to Russia and the Kremlin." She placed her hands on his knees. "So, are you proud of me, Daddy?"

Taurus stood up. He stepped past her and looked out of the window. "Baby, you just opened up a can of worms." He started to shake. His mind was racing so fast that he couldn't even think straight. He thought about all of the powers in Washington. He thought about all those shiesty, racist, egotistical, angry, vindictive people, and he knew that Natalia had no idea what he was up against.

Natalia came behind him and hugged his body. "Daddy, I know that the only reason they freed you from prison and faked your death is because they wanted you to work for them by infecting and killing off our people. I know that because they saved your life that you are indebted to them. You are not the first man that has had a connection to Russia and have gotten off from committing a serious crime. But there is also something else that you don't know." She turned him around so that he could look into her bright blue eyes.

Taurus held her face, he was still shaking. "What else, baby? What else don't I know?"

"You don't know my mother is the one that pulled the strings for you to be released. You don't know that from the moment you stepped foot out of those prison walls, I knew you were out, and every second since then I've been trying to find you for myself. I didn't kill my mother until I knew that you were free."

Taurus frowned. "So, you really did kill Nastia?"

Natalia nodded. "She raised me to believe that you were a sick and perverted man. She made me feel that the Black side of me was tainted, and because of it, that I would never be anything more than evil. She told me that I was the devil's spawn, and because of her, I grew up with a complex." She started to cry. "She hated me because I was mixed. Up there in Russia, they hated me as well. They called me names and raped me, even with my mother's knowledge. They did this under the guise of it being the Russian way. My mother wanted them to fuck the black out of me, and I hated her for it. But the more they tried, and the worse things got. All it did was make me yearn for you—my father. When I found information that told me that she was looking to get you out of prison so that you could commit genocide on your own people, and so that she could secretly be with you behind the

Kremlin's back, I snapped. I don't regret it because all I've ever wanted was you." Natalia kissed his lips and shook her head. "He's no longer in debt to Putin. It cost me more than four hundred million, and don't ask me where I got it from, but it's paid. You are no longer in debt to the White House, and he is no longer in debt to Putin. We are free, and once again all I want is you." She hugged him.

Taurus hugged her back and rested his chin on top of her head. "Damn, baby, you did all of that for yo' daddy?" He was at a loss for words.

She nodded. "Yes. I exhausted a lot of resources, and I am low now, but I don't care. All I want is you, and you are all that matters to me, outside of Junior."

Jahliyah pushed open the door and placed her hand on her hip. "Well, here y'all go again. What type of party are y'all having around this piece?"

Natalia backed off Taurus and shot daggers at Jahliyah. "Don't you know how to knock?"

Jahliyah ignored her. "Daddy, this is what you're doing now? You're fuckin' with your own daughter on some sick shit? Really?"

Natalia hurried and stood within Jahliyah's face. "Listen to me, Jahliyah, you don't have the slightest clue of what you're dealing with, but if I was you, I would back up and leave while your life is still intact."

Jahliyah took her earrings out of her ears. "Look, I know I come off all demure and shit, but what you fail to realize is that I was born and raised in Orange Mound. I had my first fight when I was eight years old, and I ain't lost one yet. Bitch, you're about to find out real fast that I am my mother's daughter." She placed her earrings in her pocket and pushed Natalia as hard as she could out of her face. "Get the fuck out of my face."

Natalia flew backward over the bed and wound up on her back. She bonked her head on the floor and holler out in pain. "Bitch!"

Taurus jumped in the middle of them. "What the fuck is wrong with you two? Y'all are sisters!"

Jahliyah pointed at Natalia as she got up off the floor. "Tell her that. She's the one that keeps coming at me all disrespect-fully and shit. I don't care what y'all got going on. That doesn't got shit to do wit' me. You're my father too, and I love you." She hugged him.

Once again, Phoenix stood at a safe distance while he watched the scene unfold. At its duration, he had plans to move on Taurus. First, he would lure him into a vulnerable space, and then he and his Duffle Bag Cartel would torture him until he gave up all of his wealth. Once that goal was achieved, Phoenix had visions of making Taurus pay the ulti-mate penalty. His legacy would be no more, and finally, Phoe-nix would reign as the sole king of the Stevens family and its bloodline.

Natalia was both embarrassed and infuriated. She saw Jahliyah wrap her arms around Taurus, and she snapped. She slipped her hand under the mattress of the bed and grabbed her .9 millimeter.

"You trying to take my daddy away from me, bitch? Well, that ain't happening. Over my dead body."

She jumped up with the gun in her hand and anger flowing through her veins. She aimed the gun at Jahliyah and squeezed.

***

Rondo and twenty cars pulled up to the back of Phoenix's mansion and jumped out of their cars, heavily armed. Rondo kept the shotgun pressed into the back of Jimmy Bands' head as he guided him to the back door of the mansion. He had already stripped him of his millions and now Phoenix was next. Rondo was hungry for the crown and was ready to meet death to obtain it. "Keep walking, bitch nigga. We almost there."

Jimmy Bands kept his hands in the air. "I'm doing everythang you tell me to. All I ask is that you don't kill me."

Skyy kicked Jimmy in his ass. "Shut up, bro. I ain't never known yo' ass to be this soft."

"Bitch, I'm yo' brother, and dis how you do me? Where is your loyalty?" Jimmy asked, hurt.

Rondo laughed. "A bitch gon' always be loyal to the money. Never forget that." He tossed Jimmy Bands through the back door of the mansion just as two shots went off upstairs.

"What the fuck?" Skyy hollered, falling to the ground.

Ghost

Chapter 3

Natalia aimed the gun at Jahliyah and squeezed the trigger. *Boom!*

Taurus pushed Jahliyah on the bed before the slug could rip into her. He spun and dove, tackling Natalia to the floor but not before her gun could let off a second round. He took a hold of her wrist and slammed it against the floor until she released her grip on the gun, dropping it. Natalia struggled against him. Jahliyah scooted all the way backward up against the headboard looking herself over to make sure she hadn't been hit.

"Let me up, Daddy. I'm sick of this bitch already. I'm about to kill her ass." She groaned as she fought against his hold.

Taurus applied more of his weight to her. "That's yo' ma-fuckin' sister. What the hell is wrong wit' you girl?"

Jahliyah jumped out of the bed and rushed over to pick up the gun. She tightened both hands around it and aimed it down at Natalia. "I should kill you right now. I should empty the clip on yo' evil."

Taurus looked up at his second daughter perplexed. Natalia continued to wiggle crazily to break free of him. He came to his knees somehow picking her up along with him. "Jahliyah, baby, put the gun down. This shit ain't happening."

Jahliyah shook her head as a tear slid down her cheek. "N'all Daddy, I can't. This bitch is too crazy over you. I don't know what her problem is but she just took it there with me. If I don't kill her ass she gon' find a way to come for my head. I know she will. She's fucked up in the head."

"Bitch, you fucked up. You're standing there talking all that shit and you ain't doing nothing. Pull the trigger then. Come on! Pull it! I ain't afraid of shit you're talking."

"Natalia, shut up! Please baby, don't provoke her." Taurus warned.

"*Baby?* Daddy, you're still going to call her baby after she just tried to kill me? What the fuck?" Jahliyah grew irate. She wondered if Taurus really loved her sister more than he did her. Was it because her complexion was more of a lighter tone than hers? Or maybe because they had obviously slept together on more than one occasion. For Jahliyah, shit just wasn't adding up.

"Bitch, you heard him. I *am* his baby. All his. I'll do shit for my Daddy you could never do. All you have over me is the fact that he loved your mother more than he did mine. That's it! But I'm his number one now. Me!" Natalia screamed.

Jahliyah held the gun out toward them. "Daddy, tell her to shut up! Tell her she's wrong! Please! You can't possibly love this crazy yellow bitch more than me."

Taurus grew weary. "I love both of you the same. Natalia, get off that bullshit. Why are you creating division? You two are sisters. Y'all supposed to love one another no matter what. Fuck the dumb shit." Taurus snapped, leaning back into Natalia.

"I don't give a fuck about nothing or nobody outside of you and my son. That's just what it is, Daddy. You can't force me to love this bitch. I can't and *I don't.*" Natalia said, screaming it over Taurus's shoulder.

Phoenix frowned as he stood outside of the door. He shook his head understanding Natalia's true nature and feelings. *Oh, yeah? That's how this bitch really feel? Awright then, I got a trick for all of they asses. We'll see who gets the last laugh, that's on my Duffle Bag Gang.* He slowly eased away from the door.

Before he could leave the hallway entirely, he peered over the balcony and saw Rondo slowly creeping with a shotgun pressed into the back of Jimmy Bands' head. He squinted his eyes. *Oh no. I know this lil' nigga ain't on demon time like this.* He checked his waist and found it empty. He'd left his F&N on the kitchen counter downstairs. He cursed under his breath and headed back to the bedroom where all of the commotion was taking place. He twisted the knob and eased inside of the room. Jahliyah jumped back and nearly pulled the trigger at the sight of him. "Phoenix, what the hell are you doing here?"

Phoenix placed his finger to his lips. "Shhh, it's a hit. Mafuckas in the mansion right now on some jack boy shit. My stick downstairs. I need that bitch you toting, Jahliyah, or we're about to get the bidness done to us right now, shawty."

Jahliyah backed up with the gun pointed at him. "You got me fucked up, potna. What, you thank I just stepped off the porch yesterday or somethin'? You tryna save my sister and I ain't going for it. Put yo' hands up. Now!"

Phoenix waved her off. "Shawty, on gang, on our bloodline, them mafuckas down there right now on some fuck shit. Now, gimme the damn gun. Y'all can fight over Taurus' old ass later." He held his hand out for the gun.

Natalia grabbed a .380 from her ankle holster and stood back up. She moved Taurus out of the way. "Phoenix, you bet not be lying 'cause I don't need you to save me from nobody. If I really wanted to kill Jahliyah that bitch would have been dead already, you best believe that." She hurried to the door and twisted the knob. She peeked out of it and saw the many shadows along the walls of the living room and kitchen downstairs. "Shit, he's telling the truth."

Taurus rushed to the mattress and flipped it. He grabbed two .45s from under it and tossed one of them to Phoenix. Both had fifty round magazines. Taurus nudged Natalia out of the way and eased into the hallway. "Stay in there," he whispered.

"You got me fucked up. I ride for my Daddy." Phoenix cringed. He wanted to shoot both of them out of sheer jealousy. He cocked his pistol and waited to see what Taurus and Natalia were about to do.

Jahliyah ducked on the side of the bed in fear. She knew bullets didn't have any names attached to them and she most definitely didn't want to get caught in the cross fires. She made herself as small as she possibly could along the dresser and the king-sized bed.

Rondo curled his upper lip and clenched his jaw repeatedly. He grabbed Jimmy Bands around the neck. "Say Phoenix, you bitch ass nigga! Bring yo' punk ass down those stairs and surrender, or on the Mound, I'm about to drop Jimmy soft ass in yo' shit. Break yo' mafuckin' self nigga, on bro 'nem grave."

Phoenix stepped to the banister that overlooked the downstairs. He saw Rondo give the order for his troops to head to and up the stairwell. Phoenix laughed. He counted eight men total and Skyy. Her positioning beside Rondo confused him due to the fact that she was supposed to be Jimmy Bands' sister. "Say Rondo, what dis all 'bout, shawty?"

Rondo stopped and tightened his arm around Jimmy Band's throat. "Dere you go. Fuck nigga, you know what it is. It's time for me to step out on my own on that Mound shit. I gotta feed my wolves, and you and dis nigga, Jimmy Bands, right hurr on the fuckin' menu. Run that scratch."

Phoenix laughed. "You a certified stepper huh, nigga? Yo' so dis what you want right hurr? Bitch, I'm the king of Memphis."

Rondo slung Jimmy Bands to the floor. Skyy pointed two .9s down at her brother with hatred brewing in her eyes. She was gone off Percocets and two lines of pink Mollie. Rondo mugged Phoenix and turned the shotgun up in his direction. "Shiesty Gang, bitch! Run that cheese."

Four of Rondo's men made their way up the stairs. Their eyes were pinned on Phoenix. They were sure that they had him cornered. As soon as they got two steps from the landing, Taurus slid out of the shadows and started firing. *Boom! Boom! Boom! Boom!*

Two of the men hollered out in pain right away while the other two tried to locate where the gun fire was coming from. Before they could locate the direction of the attack, five bullets ripped into their flesh, knocking them back down the steps with their brains hanging from the front of their faces. Natalia followed their bodies as they rolled down the steps, jumping over them. She started her assault on the remaining young bodyguards that started to shoot up in the direction of Phoenix. The young gunners were still oblivious to the fact that Taurus had been the initial shooter. Her bullets shredded them on contact using her military-issued cop killer rounds. They fell to the ground, and she ducked for cover.

Rondo had seen enough. He started shooting the big shotgun back to back at nothing or nobody in general. Skyy broke out of the door. Rondo backed up releasing slug after slug on the same escape mission as her.

Phoenix laughed as he watched the scene unfold. Natalia rolled around on the floor looking for a clean shot to murder Rondo. Before she could release any more slugs, Rondo ran and jumped through the patio glass doors sending glass splashing everywhere. He rolled onto his back and got up sprinting. He jumped into the awaiting Benz truck and the driver stepped on the gas.

Taurus and Natalia ran behind the vehicle for a short time sending bullet after bullet, shattering the back window. The driver swerved and somehow made it off the property after receiving one to the shoulder. He groaned out in pain. Blood leaked from his fingers as he turned on to the asphalt and stormed down the street to their retreat.

Taurus stood in the middle of the road with his tattooed chest heaving up and down. Natalia stepped beside him, her chest rising and falling just as much. Phoenix approached the pair and nodded; murderous revenge was on his agenda. He would be forced to teach Rondo a lesson. It was all a part of the game. Memphis was cutthroat and there was no way around it. While he figured out a way to crush the Shiesty gang and its leader, he would plot to completely disarm, break and find a way to make Taurus bow down to his gangsta. The Duffle Bag Cartel was only fit to have one leader in power and the way Phoenix saw it the leader had to be him. Taurus was living on borrowed time.

Natalia looked up at Taurus with concern. "Daddy, you good?"

Taurus kept his eyes on the back of Rondo's getaway truck until he could no longer see it. "Who the fuck was that?" He wanted to know, ignoring Natalia's question. He tucked his gun into the small of his back.

"That was that young nigga, Rondo." Jimmy Bands said, stepping up beside Phoenix after Jahliyah released him.

Phoenix mugged the young hustler. He stepped up to him and pressed his gun to his forehead. "You brought that fuck nigga to my house, where y family lay their head, and somehow I feel like you think this is acceptable. Bitch, explain yourself."

Jimmy Bands was over having guns pulled on him for one day. "That nigga already knew where you stayed. I ain't direct him to yo' duck off. I got way more respect for you than to ever do that so get this gun out of my face." He swiped the barrel from his forehead.

"Who brought that nigga into the fold?" Taurus asked. He walked up to Phoenix and looked him in the eye.

Phoenix glared at Jimmy Bands. "That's his homeboy. I ain't stamp that bitch nigga. I would have never done that because I would have seen the snake in his sucka ass."

Natalia looked over to Jahliyah and had the urge to slump her. She imagined killing her sister and having Taurus all to herself. The thought gave her a warm feeling deep within her belly. Now wasn't the time. She would play her cards close to her chest and take Jahliyah out when it was most intelligent to do so. She looked from Phoenix to Jimmy Bands. "Sounds like y'all got a lot of shit you need to work out. Come on, Daddy. This is their problem, it's beneath you." She took a hold of Taurus's hand making sure she locked eyes with Jahliyah as she did so. A slight smile appeared on her face.

Jahliyah felt a strong current of jealousy wash over her as she watched her hand interlock with that of her father's. She cringed, turned, and walked away from all of them. "I think it's time I head back to New York. Ain't nothing here for me no more." She took a few steps before the tears welled in her eyes, then she took off running toward the mansion.

"Jahliyah!" Taurus took off behind her.

This infuriated Natalia. "Y'all need to clean up this mess, Phoenix. This shit is ridiculous!" She jogged behind her father and sister not wanting to be left out.

Phoenix watched the trio until they disappeared, serious anger surging through him. "Jimmy, this shit is on you. I want that nigga and his gang wiped out of Memphis. Yo' bitch ass better get to it because if I have to step in I'ma slide on you first. That's on gang. Now fuck wit' it if you thank it's a game.

Come help me get rid of the dead bitches, mane, hurry the fuck up." He turned and walked away from him.

Jimmy Bands sucked his gold teeth and nodded. "I'ma have to buss that nigga Phoenix's brain. I already see how dis shit finna play out." He pulled his nose and headed back to the mansion to help dispose of the bodies there.

Chapter 4
Three weeks later

It was a sunny, yet very breezy day in south Memphis when Rondo pulled his red SRT up to Cane Creek Apartments. The small units were packed with low-income families, mostly elderly and single mothers who were on Section 8.

Though these units had previously started out with strict rules, they were now infested with low life, cold-hearted dope and jack boys who were quick to murder for a name and clout. Everywhere Rondo looked he saw men walking around with black masks and guns. The women seemed to follow the same trend. Even most of the kids were armed, and while the other children played normally, most of them were heavily armed and ready to catch a body on an opp. The Cane Creek Apartments were run by the Choppa Gang.

The crew was known for backstabbing their own members, pulling kick doors, rape, murder and so much more. The Choppa Gang was well-known all-over Memphis and very few crews had been given a pass by the clan of savages. Lucky for Rondo, the Cane Creek Apartments and the Choppa Gang was run by his older brother, Marpooh, but every dope boy and animal in the city referred to his brother simply as Pooh.

When Pooh saw his little brother roll up and pull inside of the massive parking lot that connected most of the units in Cane Creek, he hopped out of the black van where he'd been sitting with a Draco on his lap preparing for an opp to try their luck at rolling through his trenches on some dumb shit. He glided up to Rondo's open driver's window and lowered his black half mask that shielded much of his face. "What it do, baby bruh? Fuck took you so long to slide through?" Pooh nodded at Skyy as she sat in the passenger's seat with two pink

.9 millimeters with black handles on her lap. "Who dat is right thurr?"

Rondo got out of the SRT and tucked his Glock .9 into the waistband of his Amir jeans. "Dats my bitch right thurr. She good people. Quit salivating at the mouth 'bout my shawty too, nigga." Rondo nudged him.

Pooh ignored him and stuck his head into the open driver's window. He saw the way Skyy's Fendi skirt rose above her succulent thick caramel thighs and the aroma of her perfume seemed to call out for him. "Say, how you doin' miss lady? My brother treating you right and all dat shit?"

Skyy lowered her pink Cartier wood frames and peered over the top of them at him. "Yeah, playboy. My lil' daddy handles his bidness. What's it to you tho?" The sunlight shined off of the Kylie Jenner gloss concoction that was splayed upon her juicy lips.

Pooh pulled out fifty thousand dollars in rubber bands. "You see what dat is right thurr? I change bitchez lives round dis way. You just rolling through the south, shawty, you better get a load of what the fuck I got going on. Usually, when a bitch rolls up into these parking ways, she gotta kiss the ring, and I ain't talking 'bout no jewelry." He clutched his piece.

Skyy held up her fingers that were bright with three carats or better of flawless diamonds. "Shawty, I don't fuck around wit' the south like that. Dis dat southeast shit over hurr though. Orange Mound all day every day, and the Kang of that is my mister that's standing out there mugging yo' ass right now." She laughed, "that's the only nigga's rang I'm kissing."

"The Kang?" Pooh took a step back and looked Rondo up and down. "Fuck you looking all crazy fo'?"

Rondo side stepped his blatant attempt at disrespect. "Look Mane, I need to holler at you on some real shit. All dis other childish shit can wait for another day."

Pooh looked him over from the corners of his eyes. "Dis talk gon' lead to me putting some bread in my Choppa Gang's pockets?"

Rondo nodded, "you muthafuckin' right."

"Den you awready know you got my attention. Let me set up my security so we can go and chop it up." He stuck his head back into the window. "Say lil' bitch, on gang, I got a gee say you let me fuck that pussy for an hour. Two gees if you let me hit that fat ass, I know you sitting on. What you thank 'bout that?"

Skyy's pussy jumped. She had never had a man come at her right in front of her nigga before, and to be throwing so much money her way for a slice of her cat was enough to label her intrigued. She would have to research Pooh a bit more, and then find a way to go around Rondo to see what he was really all about. "Shawty my nigga standing right thurr. You ain't gon' respect his slot?"

Pooh frowned, "dis ain't no mafuckin' Orange Mound. Bitch, this is Crane Creek. Choppa Gang, I'm the Kang round dis mafucka, so what it is?"

"Damn," Skyy looked out at Rondo, afraid to say the wrong thing. "Babe?"

Rondo placed his hand on Pooh's shoulder. "Say gang, how 'bout we talk bidness first and then we can see what's to shawty after that."

Pooh eyed her juicy thighs again. "Yeah, I guess that's cool, but I don't give a fuck what nam one of y'all talking 'bout, I gotta have shawty ass, if only for a night." He winked at her and threw ten thousand dollars in her lap. "Bitch, you owe me and I don't accept returns." He placed his arm around Rondo's neck, "bitch let's talk dat bidness then." They walked away from the car.

Skyy grabbed the money and thumbed through it with a smile on her face after seeing that it was mostly hundreds with a few fifties. *Who was this Pooh nigga from Crane Creek and why is he on my heels like this?* She looked around the parking lot and saw all kinds of beautiful women walking around scantily clad. There were a bunch of shirtless men as well with big guns sticking out of their waistbands. She noted a group of females with black bandanas covering their faces mugging her and whispering to each other. She rolled up Rondo's windows and sat behind the five percent tint. *Damn I gotta do my research.* Her phone vibrated for the tenth time that day. She saw Jimmy Bands' face come across the screen. He was trying once again to contact her through the What's App. She ignored the call and tucked the phone into her Birkin bag alongside of the money. She was still unsure of how she was going to face him but in time she felt it would be inevitable.

Rondo waited until they were inside one of the apartments that was used for whipping large quantities of heroin before he took a seat across from Pooh and spilled the beans. "I'm beefing wit' that nigga Jimmy Bands and I gotta execute his bitch ass before I climb that ladder and fuck over Phoenix. I'm coming for Orange Mound and if you help me pull dis shit off, we can merge. I'm willing for the Shiesty Gang to fall under Choppa Gang as long as I can sit equally on the throne beside you."

Pooh laughed, "boy, you my little brother. Orange Mound can't be seeing no more than a million a day. We see dat shit over here before twelve. Dis shit doesn't sound like a benefit to me shawty. How much cheese you tryna put up for this endeavor?"

Rondo was only sitting on three million in cash and that was before he was set to pay all his workers in the streets. Imagining how much money Pooh was making suddenly made him insecure. "Damn nigga, we got the same momma and the same daddy. I'm yo' lil' brother, don't dat shit stand for any thang?"

"Bitch, if it don't make dollars it don't make sense. You already know I'm slimed in. That sibling shit dead to me so either make this shit sound more appealing or I'ma have to pass, shawty. What can you offer me, cause dem Duffle Bag Boys play fa keeps?"

Rondo couldn't believe that he was forced to go above and beyond to prove himself to Pooh, the fact that they were brothers in his mind meant that Pooh should have been down to help him fully take over Orange Mound. "Say shawty you already got this Cane Creek shit on lock, right?"

"You damn skippy, my nigga, me and Three-O. We've had this bitch locked down ever since we were twelve years old, and my Daddy caught that sentence. What that got to do wit' anythang though?"

Rondo lowered his eyes and looked off across the wide parking lot where a bunch of people were roaming back and forth. "What if when I took over the Mound I gave you forty percent of it, and its Geekers. That way Cane Creek would reach from the south all the way through the southeast. That's a whole lot of land mass to do with whatever you please."

Pooh rubbed his chin, "what else you got to go along with that lil one?"

"Damn nigga, what more do you want?" Rondo was starting to get irritated.

"I been hearing that nigga Taurus back in Memphis, mane. Mafuckas say he rolling in the dough and I want all of that shit. I got a couple connects below the border who said if a mafucka brings his head to them on a platter, it's worth five million alone, and his daughter, Natalia, is worth the same price. That's ten million, bitch. Five'll go to the Slimes and five'll go to the vault. That's talking that shit right thurr. If you want the Choppa Gang to stand behind you, fuck wit' me on dat level."

Rondo nodded in deep thought. He'd heard a lot about the legend Taurus Stevens over the years. His name rang bells all over Memphis. Most of the young hustlers in the slums aspired to be just like him. Rondo didn't know the first step to getting close to the kingpin. "Check dis out, mane, and I ain't gon' lie, I don't know how to get close to that nigga but I'm about to find out really quick. Question is, if I get up wit' him and deliver him to you, you gon' crush Jimmy Bands and Phoenix and help me flip the Duffle Bag Cartel and Orange Mound over to the Shiesty Gang, making it one hundred percent mine, or are you still looking for a cut of my turf?"

Pooh waved him off as his mouth twisted into a sardonic smile. "N'all nigga, fuck Orange Mound. This Cane Creek, baby. That's all I care about right thurr." *I'ma drop yo' lil' ass as soon as you hit that stature anyway,* Pooh thought, *blood or no blood.*

"Okay, cool. Well, let me figure this shit out and I'll get back to you. In the meantime, I need some artillery. I brought cash, and I need for you to reach."

Pooh smiled, "bitch, you bought cash. That's all you had to say. It's good; follow me." He placed his arm around Rondo's neck and walked him into the building trying his best to hide the smirk. *It's all good bitch nigga.*

Chapter 5

Natalia sat across from both Taurus and Jahliyah as he took an ice pack and held it on to Jahliyah's head. Jahliyah's eyes were closed. She felt sick as a dog and her vision continuously went blurry. Natalia bounced on her toes as she sat growing more and more irritated.

"Baby, is this helping at all?" Taurus looked down at her and adjusted the ice pack a bit more.

Jahliyah nodded, "yeah, my head is not pounding as much as it was before. Thank you, Daddy."

"It's all good." Taurus wrapped his arm around her shoulders and brought closer to him.

Jahliyah rested her head on his chest. The intoxicating scent of his cologne gave her a sense of peace. Her migraine slowly began to diminish. She smiled and started to drift off.

Natalia hopped up, "Daddy, she's asleep. Let me help her go upstairs so she can lay in the bed. I need to talk to you about somethin'."

Jahliyah opened her eyes. "Here we go wit' this shit."

Taurus took a deep breath and slowly blew it out. "Look, y'all lil' asses ain't 'bout to keep dis beefing shit up. Y'all sisters and I'll take *both* of you out the game before I let y'all keep fighting. I ain't playing either."

"You ain't even gotta do that. All you gotta do is let us put her on a private flight back to New York, matter fact, private may be a bit too much for her seeing as she ain't never lived that sort of lifestyle before. We wouldn't want to shock her system so badly that it kills her." She crossed her arms and laughed.

"That's it," Jahliyah stood up and mugged Natalia. "What I thank you should do, Daddy, is let me and her go at each other for five minutes. The winner gets to do whatever she wants to and the other one has to disappear for good. She thank she so tough and all that. All we gotta do is see."

Natalia stood up and blew a razor blade into her hand. She held it up as it gleamed in the living room. "One thang is for sho' and that's you ain't got no wins with me. I have literally murdered bitchez like you before I was fifteen years old. Your death would be a delight. Now play wit' it." She slipped the blade back into her mouth. "Daddy, we need to talk, *now!*"

Jahliyah shook her head, "if fucking with Taurus on that level got you acting all like this I'm glad that we never have crossed those lines. That white shit that's mixed with our bloodline inside of you got you trippin'."

"Bitch, everybody's blood is mixed up, I'm probably blacker than you are." Natalia spat.

"Yeah, that sounds logical." Jahliyah rolled her eyes.

"Just listen to y'all asses. Y'all sound immature as hell. I can't believe this shit." He looked back and forth from one daughter unto the next. "When will this shit end?"

"Daddy, I didn't get any ample time to spend with you. All I have is my mother's diary. She wrote about you. She said that you were the love of her life. She said that no man has ever made her feel like you did, and that no one has ever loved her as much as you did. I just want to get to know my father. I'm not asking for anything else. Can we please take some time to get to know each other?" Jahliyah asked.

"When do you leave?" Natalia hollered as she clenched her fists. She hated the thought of Taurus having always loved Princess the most, and that her own mother was nothing more than a snow bunny that he'd slipped up and gotten pregnant. *This bitch has got to go.*

"For your information, my offices are officially closed due to the new strain of COVID circulating around the United States from overseas. The Delta variant is extremely lethal, and until they get a grasp on it, I will be working virtually. The things that are being asked of me can be done from a computer, so I am free to be here to get to know my father. I don't care how it makes you feel." Jahliyah said dismissively.

Natalia lowered her head and eyes and shot daggers at Jahliyah. "Bitch, the only reason you still have breath inside of your lungs is because of our father, that's it. I don't take too kindly to competition."

"And I don't take too kindly to threats. You must not know who my mother was?" Jahliyah stepped forward. "You ain't the only one that got that on-go shit in your blood. The shit you talkin' don't spook me."

Natalia's heart began to pound in her chest as she imagined killing Jahliyah in cold blood. A devilish grin crept across her round face. "Okay, Jahliyah. You win. Taurus, I'm out of here. You can have your fuckin' daughter who looks just like you. You will never have to worry about me or Junior ever again!" She stomped her feet and took off toward the upstairs of the mansion.

Taurus closed his eyes as he massaged his throbbing temples. "This shit is worse than Blaze and Princess. I don't know how much more of this I can really take."

Jahliyah walked up to him and laid her head on his chest, wrapping her arms around his neck. "Daddy, I'll play nice for you. We shouldn't be arguing. You are one hundred percent right, and the last thing I want is for you to be stressed out when we just met. I'll play nice. You have my word." She stepped back on her tippy toes.

Taurus kissed her lips, and then her forehead. "Baby, that would make me so happy. There is so much I want to do with you, but it won't be possible if the two of you are constantly at each other's throats every day. You gon' hold me down?"

"That depends; am I your favorite baby girl?" She batted her long eyelashes and popped back on her legs.

She was the spit image of her mother. Taurus's heart leaped, reminiscing about the times he and Princess shared. "You know I can't trip myself up like that, but your mother was my everything. My first and only love, and you are her twin. That's all I can say." He winked at her.

Jahliyah sucked on her bottom lip and smiled. "That's enough for me. You can go to her evil ass now." She kissed his lips again and headed towards the kitchen, her tight shorts creeping into the crack of her supple ass. *Damn*, Taurus quickly glanced away, not wanting to taint the image of the only daughter he hadn't touched.

Taurus entered the bedroom as Natalia was packing her Louis Vuitton suitcases talking to herself. He eased inside of the room and closed the door behind himself. "Baby, what are you doing?"

"Don't call me baby. You don't have the right to do that anymore." She opened the huge closet and grabbed a handful of the clothes, yanking them from the hangers, tossing them onto the bed.

Taurus eased behind her and pulled her close to him. "I don't give a fuck what's going on between you and your sister, I ain't about to let you go nowhere. I just got you back into my life. I ain't about to lose you already."

"Let me go, Taurus. I don't want shit else to do with you. I get it. She's your complexion. She has deeper dimples than me. You loved her mother the most. I don't measure up. I regret even finding you. I'm always the last on everybody's list to be loved. I just thought with my actual father things would be different but who am I kidding?" She started to pry his hands off her.

As soon as they were loose, Taurus grabbed a hold of her and slammed her into the wall. "What the fuck you want from me, Natalia? Is this what you want?" He sunk his teeth into her exposed neck, sucking her delicate skin into his mouth. He yanked her tight Fendi skirt up to her hips. His hand ventured inside of her panties rubbing her pussy that started to leak as soon she felt his middle digit enter her hot, tight hole.

"Mmm-Daddy let me go. I hate you right now." She spaced her thighs.

Taurus started fingering her at full speed with two digits. Natalia creamed all over them. He licked all over her lips and down her neck. "You belong to me Natalia. You my lil baby, and I'm show yo' ass what the fuck I mean." He turned her around and forced her to put her hands on the door as if she was about to be searched. He yanked her panties down and rubbed his big dick head up and down her crease, before sinking eleven inches deep into her coochie.

"Daddddddeeeeeeeee!" Taurus took a hold of her hips and proceeded to fucking her hard. "You ain't going nowhere! You're my baby girl. I need you. I'll kill a mafucka over you! You come from me!"

Natalia shuddered as she took the pounding. Her tongue licked all over her lips. She slammed back into him and struggled to catch her breath. "Daddy. Daddy. Daddy, shit, slow down. You're too deep, unnnnnn, shit!"

Taurus pulled her back so that she could bend all the way over, once she was at the perfect angle, he really got to tearing her tight pussy up. He loved to watch his dick go in and out of her. He still couldn't believe that she was his baby, and that she was so fine. Guilt came over him, but he pushed it into the back of his mind. He understood that this act was how Natalia wanted to be loved, that it was the only way he could show her that she meant the world to him, at least that's what he told himself to justify the fact that he was fuckin' his own baby girl and loving every stroke of it.

"Unnnnnn, daddy!" Natalia pinched her clitoris and came all over Taurus. Her knees buckled. She fell to the ground.

Taurus picked her up and carried her to the bed. He balled her up and laid on top of her once his dick was fully embedded inside of her vagina again. He long stroked her while he breathed hard. "You ain't going nowhere! You hear me? I need you. You ain't going nowhere away from Daddy. Say it."

Natalia was in tears after cumming for the third time. She felt Taurus diving deeply into her box over and over. Every time he wound up in her stomach she groaned and ran her fingers over his lips. He sucked them. "I ain't going nowhere, Daddy. Please. I promise. Aww, shit. I'm not. I love youuuuuuuuuuuuuu!"

Taurus tightened his grip and started to fuck her so hard that the headboard began slamming into the wall with a steady *tap, tap, tap* sound. There was a huge puddle of secretions under their sexing bodies. Both were moaning and groaning. The scent of their coupling along with the audio brought Jahliyah upstairs to the door. She placed her ear to it and listened.

"You're my Daddy. You're my Daddy. Fuck me, Daddy. Fuck yo' baby. Unnnnnn, shit. Fuck yo' baby girlllllllllll! I'm cummiiiinnnggggg!"

Jahliyah took her ear away from the door and placed it back. She listened a second longer and stomped her foot. Why, why, why? She was starting to feel like that since both Taurus and Natalia had a sexual relationship that it was going to cause her father to love her far less than he did her sister. She felt sick to the stomach. She placed her hand around the door handle ready to break up the sexing pair but the sounds of Phoenix pulling into the driveway inside of his Hellcat stopped her.

She stood there for a moment wondering if she should allow for the two to be caught. A sly smile splayed across her face.

Ghost

Chapter 6

When Phoenix opened the front door, he had two Duffle bags that were filled with a total of three million dollars. He was shocked to find Jahliyah standing in the doorway wearing a pair of coochie cutter jean shorts and a tight tank top that broadcasted her C cup titties to the max. Her nipples were prominent through the material and after hearing and smelling her sister and father upstairs they were erect. Phoenix scooted past her.

Jahliyah closed the door. "Damn cuz, what's the matter, you can't speak?" She stepped back in front of him and popped back on her legs.

Phoenix could smell the sex in the air. He sniffed a bit harder and looked toward the upper portion of the house. "What up shawty, where my baby mama at?"

Jahliyah nodded her head upstairs. "She up dat way. What you looking for her fo'?"

"Taurus up there, too?" He dropped the bags to the floor.

"Yop, they both up there talking or chilling, I guess. Ain't my bidness and ain't my problem. What you got in these bags?"

Phoenix became disgruntled. "Money; the only thang a mafucka should be putting in these bags is that cake. Pose to be three million. I gotta pull out my money machine to make sho' doe, you wanna help me?"

"Shid, is you giving me some of it?" Jahliyah was dead serious.

Phoenix laughed, "crazy how you can ask me fo' some cash but you ain't even gave me a hug yet. What type of time is yo' lil' ass on?" He looked into her eyes, challenging her.

Jahliyah twisted her face into a smirk. "You always on somethin', boy get yo' ass over hurr and get you a hug."

Phoenix slipped into her embrace and took a hold of that meaty ass. He cuffed the glutes and sucked all over her neck. "Damn Jahliyah, you're so mafuckin' fine. They ain't making too many hoez down here in Memphis like dis no mo." He sniffed her up and down and got hard from the closeness of her.

Jahliyah allowed him to feel all over her lower region until he unbuttoned her jeans. When he slipped his hand inside of them and separated her pussy lips with his middle finger she backed up. "Boy we cousins, I keep telling you that I don't get down like that."

Phoenix sucked his fingers into his mouth and shivered. "Jahliyah, let's keep this shit all the way real, you already know how our family gets down. I'm tryna see what's good between those thighs even if I gotta pay for that shit. So how much is it gon' take." He stepped up into her space again taking a hold of her by the backside. He loved that juicy booty.

Jahliyah looked into his eyes and laughed. Her deep dimples enticed him all the more. "Phoenix, you just don't get it. We're family. Blood! That means we share the same DNA. How could we ever cross the line like that?"

Phoenix dropped down and licked the crotch of her jeans. He turned her around and licked all over her ass cheeks, sniffing her crease. "I don't give a fuck about none of that. We're cousins, and this is Memphis. Everybody down here fuckin' somebody in they family on the low, I know that for a fact. Just thank 'bout what they up thurr doing. I ain't no mafuckin' goofy by a long shot."

Jahliyah laughed, "so, what that got to do wit' me? Maybe my standards are different than my half-sisters."

Phoenix walked her backwards until she was up against the refrigerator. "You mean to tell me that Taurus ain't never got a hold of this pussy before?" He rubbed it through the jeans once again noting the fact that all of Taurus's daughters had fat pussies. It was like a right of passage it seemed.

"Hell n'all, I would never fuck my own Daddy, ugh, what type of shit is that?"

Phoenix pinched her sex lips together and squeezed them. "I don't know if I believe that. I know that shit we got going on inside of our blood, and I know how Taurus get down. He been fuckin' my baby mama ever since she found his ass. We ain't fucked since. You are two times as cold as she is, with way more ass and titties. You got these deep dimples and thangs, and plus that walk on you is mean. I can't see that nigga not getting all up in dis ass, and to be quite honest I couldn't blame him. Even if you were my shawty I don't thank I'd be able to keep my hands off you." He slid his finger into her booty hole and bit into her neck at the same time.

Jahliyah imagined Taurus doing that to her and shuddered. She pushed Phoenix back. "Well, I ain't going. I just wanna be loved by my Daddy in the natural way. You're my cousin, I ain't crossing those lines with you. Deal with it." She turned and walked away from him on weak knees. As soon as she got to the bathroom, she locked the door and fell to the floor with her thighs wide open and her jean shorts thrown in the corner. In less than five minutes, she'd brought herself to two screaming orgasms while she bit down on a towel.

***

Jimmy Bands took his razor blade and chopped through the pile of heroin, creating four thick lines. He took them one at a time, coughing. He scooted back on the couch and closed his eyes inside of the big den. Beside the residue of the heroin was ten large towers of cash all around the table. It was his two days take from the narcotic sales all throughout the slums of Clover Land in Houston, Harris County and Dallas. When it was all done and counted, his total would come to two million and five hundred thousand.

MayBaby stepped into the den with a small bottle of Ducè. She drank from it and struggled to keep her eyes open. She was gone off of Percocets and Xanax. She slowly made her way over until she was standing in front of him. She kicked his Yeezys. "You got somebody at the doe up thurr that wanna speak to you and I thank it's in our best interest that you do so."

"So now you thanking for me?" Jimmy Bands asked without opening his eyes.

"I said *us*. I ain't trying to get into no huge argument wit' yo' ass. You need to trust me on dis one."

Jimmy Bands sat up and scratched his inner thigh, and then his arms. He was regretting taking the Percocets now, the heroin was already strong enough to get him to where he needed to be. "Who da fuck is it shawty, got damn, I'm tryna get in my mode and thangs."

"Yeah; I'm tryna make sho' you don't get us killed in the process. The nigga that wanna holler at you is up there in rank and from what I hear—he got a whole deck full of grimy cutthroat niggas that war with Cartels just for the fun. My bitchez done told me through their pillowtalk with niggaz all over Memphis that the Duffle Bag Cartel done come upon the most hated and hunted list. So yeah playboy, holler at this nigga."

Jimmy Bands snatched the bottle of Ducè out of her hand. "Bitch, go get the nigga. Make sho' you pat his ass down before he comes down hurr. Have the fellas be on point. Hurry the fuck up."

"Excuse yo' rude ass?" MayBaby stepped up to him with her hands on her hips.

Jimmy Bands gave her the look of death. He towered over her and yanked her to his chest. "'Bitch what the fuck I say do? Huh? Fuck is you still standing right her for?"

MayBaby swallowed her spit in terror before she slapped his hands up off of her. "Nigga get the fuck up off me. Who you thank you is?"

Slap!

Jimmy Bands backhanded her so hard she dropped to one knee. He grabbed her up by her hair and placed his lips on her ear. "On gang bitch I'll blow yo muthafuckin' head off if you ever try some dumb shit like that with me again. I don't know what the fuck you thank this is now ever since that youngin' done tried a pimp but don't get shit twisted." He slung her to the floor.

MayBaby bounced right back up and nodded her head up and down. "Okay Jimmy, I see you nigga. You can put those filthy ass hands on me but when those niggaz come on that bidness yo ass nut up. It's cool."

"Bitch, shut that shit up. Rondo living on borrowed time, and you know it. Now take yo' punk ass upstairs and let my company in after you give my niggaz their security detail. Beat it bitch." He flopped down on the couch and turned up his bottle of codeine.

MayBaby stood there for a second in defiance. She laughed to herself and rubbed her hands together. "Yeah, awright nigga."

When she opened the door, Three-O stood with two Crane Creek killas behind him. "Say shawty I don't usually wait this long to talk to a nigga that been placed on plate. Luckily for him, he got somebody as fine as you, answering the door or else his ass would have been blown to smithereens already. Fuck dat nigga at?"

MayBaby looked Three-O up and down from the corners of her eyes. He downstairs in the den. He's waiting for you, but I'm sorry yo' click can't go wit' you."

"What, dis Choppa Gang's president right hurr? Everywhere I go, my secret service must go. If my team of shooters ain't sliding wit' me in the daytime when it's supposed to be peace talks, then I'ma make sure they slide wit' me tonight when we come to blow some shit up, that's on gang. Which one it's gon' be?" The dark-skinned stocky animal said with his low haircut and deep waves. He was already dressed in black with a mean scowl on his face.

MayBaby shook her head and held up a finger. "Wait a minute I'll be right back. Let me make sure that it's good."

"You know what Shawty just tell that nigga Jimmy Bands that he just got put on the menu by the gang. Good luck on wiggling his way out of this one cause every nigga in my clan see red and gon' be on go to every thang Duffle Bag. Send him that message." He yanked her to him, she yelped, he kissed her lips hard and pushed her away making his departure.

Jimmy Bands came to the door just as Three-O was headed back to his line of black Bentley trucks with the Georgia tags. "Say Mane, I know dat ain't Three-O."

Three-O stopped in his tracks and turned around. His shooters clutched their weapons and mugged Jimmy Bands. Three-O started walking back to Jimmy Bands' porch. "Say potna, a contract for your head just came across our table. Mafuckas want you out the way and how I been treated so far, I ain't seeing no reason not to slump yo' bitch ass along with every thang Duffle Bag. Convince me not to or the surgery begins." After saying this, four more of Three-O's shooters pulled up on Ducatis. They had SK assault rifles on their hips.

They kicked the stands on their bikes and stood at a safe firing distance.

Jimmy Bands already knew what it was, and he wasn't crazy. "Aw shit, homey step inside and we can work this out. Come right this way."

"What about my niggaz. That bitch said n'all." Three-O snapped and pointed at MayBaby.

MayBaby stood tall, "nigga, rules are rules."

Jimmy Bands took MayBaby's neck and slammed her against the door headfirst busting her open and knocking the wind out of her. She collapsed and was knocked out cold. "Fuck what she hollering she don't know no better, now like I said right this way."

Ghost

Chapter 7

Three-O picked up MayBaby and carried her into the house. He laid her on the couch, took his Burberry handkerchief and dabbed at the blood that was leaking from the corners of her mouth. She opened her eyes, wincing in pain. He felt sympathetic. "Damn shawty, that's my fault, I hope you awright, I ain't know this crazy ass nigga was gon' fuck you up like that." He eyed Jimmy Bands.

Jimmy Bands stood with his chin tilted upward. Two of Three-O's men had him hemmed up against the living room's wall with black Dracos pressed into his Adam's Apple. The four shooters that Jimmy Bands had for security were also hemmed up. Jimmy Bands felt stupid and lower than scum. "Say bruh, I ain't never come over to Cane Creek and try to tell y'all how to handle y'all women. Dis how we get down in the south, a bitch gotta get put in her place, mane."

Three-O mugged him over his shoulder, "say, fuck nigga, I grew up watching my old man beat the fuck out of my mama. That shit ain't cool by a long shot. I ain't about to condone this dumb shit. If shawty was from the southeast like the rest of my sistas over dat way, they'd be wearing your T-shirt already out dis way, that's on gang."

Jimmy Band wanted to say something slick but decided against it. Instead, he locked eyes with MayBaby. "Shawty tell this nigga that you good so we can handle dis bidness and they can get the fuck out of my house. That's how I feel about now."

MayBaby groaned as she struggled to sit up. She held her bruised ribs. "I'm good Three-O. Y'all can let him go, please. Ain't like this the first time I got my ass whooped. I should have known better."

Three-O stood up and helped her to her feet. He kissed the back of her hand. "Say Shawty you wanna stay over her dealing wit this nigga, or do you wanna come fuck wit' the Choppa Gang, Kill Branch section?"

MayBaby had to admit that the offer sounded glorious even though she didn't fully understand for sure what it entailed. "N'all, I'm good, playboy. I love my man and thangs." She hated Jimmy Bands with a passion, but he represented her financial security and stability. He was all that she knew. The thought of stepping outside of him was terrifying.

"Awright then, suit yourself. That's a damn shame too 'cause you remind me a lot of my ol' girl. That's the first thang I thought when you opened that doe back thurr. I said shawty looks just like my mama." He smiled briefly and then mugged Jimmy Bands. "Keep yo mafuckin' hands off dis Queen my nigga. Only pussy niggaz hit women for no reason." He gave the signal for Jimmy Bands to be released. They dropped him to the floor and kept the assault rifles pointed at him.

Jimmy Bands dusted his clothes off and tried as hard as he could to not allow for Three-O to detect his irritation. He simply nodded and pulled a Newport out of his pack lighting it. "Gone upstairs and get yo' self together, MayBaby. I gotta handle some bidness down here. I'll be up there in a minute."

MayBaby got up and followed his commands. With every step that she took she could feel her ribs feeling like they had been shattered. I gotta go to the hospital, she thought, this nigga done broke my damn ribs. She slowly made her way up the stairs feeling breathless.

Jimmy Bands led the crew of savages to the den and gave Three-O the best couch seat. He handed him a bottle of Ducè and slid a plate of heroin and cocaine in front of him. "Boy or girl, both are of the purest quality."

"Never partake in liquor and drugs from the enemy, that shit will always leave you twisted in the end. I ain't fuckin' wit chu." Three-O shook up his Visine bottle that was mixed with both heroin and water. He emitted a drip and sniffed it up into each nostril before tilting his head back and sniffing hard. Once the drug began to slide down the back of his throat he sat forward and mugged Jimmy Bands. "The Rebirth my nigga, that's what I wanna talk about."

Jimmy Bands nodded, "awright what about it?"

"The Duffle Bag Cartel is set to be dismantled and destroyed starting with your chapter, and Cane Creek has been given the contract. The only way you bitch niggas gon' wiggle up out of this one is if you can deliver me a hundred bricks of that Rebirth shit that put Phoenix and Smoke on the map. That's what I want and that's what I'ma get or shit about to get ugly."

Jimmy Bands frowned. "Nigga, what makes you thank I can get you a hundred bricks just like that?"

"I don't know if you can or not but it's in your best interest to figure out how to do so. You still plugged in to that nigga Phoenix, right? At least that's what the word is all over Memphis." Three-O popped the Ducè and started to down it.

"I fucks wit', bruh, but what the fuck that got to do wit' any thang?" Jimmy needed a fix. His high was lowering, and it was becoming increasingly hard for him to control his temper.

"Well, everybody knows Phoenix is the true head of the Duffle Bag Cartel and that through his family, they've been pushing that Rebirth shit inside of Memphis for as long as the late nineties. Since den, a mafucka still ain't been able to come up with a drug as strong or addicting as that shit thurr. You mafuckas done got stupid rich and I thank it's time for the southeast to get some of that currency. The only question is how are you about to make this happen?"

Jimmy Bands shook his head, "nigga, do you know what a hundred bricks of the Rebirth is worth on the street?"

"Nope, and that shit doesn't matter to me 'cause it'll be free. Pure profit." Three-O stood up. "That's my final offer, my nigga. Either you make that shit happen or we can kick off a war. One you ain't never seen before. Kill Branch don't play no games either, but I'm sho' you already know dat."

Kill Branch was a deadly crew of low life savages who held very little regard for life theirs or anybody else's. They were headed by Three-O, and he ran them like a Black Adolf Hitler. The crew had started off with just a few young, hungry teens, but now as it stood, they were every bit of two hundred strong and causing terror all over Memphis. The fact that they were clicked in with the Choppa Gang was enough to give most cartel the jitters. Everybody knew that it was impossible to make large sums of money and war at the same time. Because Kill Branch solely specialized in the war department of the streets the narcotic sales that other cartels and gangs depended on didn't mean anything to them and they doted on that reality.

"Look bruh, I'll do what I can. When are you tryna have dis shit by?" Jimmy Bands was defeated and already plotting in his mind on the next move.

"I'll give you a few weeks seeing as that's such a big load. In the meantime, run me fifty gees so I can take my killas out on the town. That number sounds just about right." Three-O said, eyeing the table full of money and dope. He figured he'd eye balled at least fifty gees and wanted to make a statement to Jimmy Bands and his own crew of cutthroats to allow for them to see that he was in charge.

Jimmy Bands flared his nostrils. He stood up and hollered to MayBaby directing her to bring him that sum exactly. She came a few minutes later with the money inside of a Ziploc bag. She tossed it to Jimmy Bands. Jimmy Bands took the money and gave it to Three-O. "Here nigga. Now, let me walk y'all to the door."

Three-O tossed the money over his shoulder and one of his shooters caught it. He stepped before MayBaby and took her hand kissing the back of it. "I'ma catch you on the rebound shawty. It's fucked up that I gotta leave you here, but I can't make the right decision for you. But if ever you wanna come from under this toxic situation, just find me. Everybody knows who Three-O is. Awright, lil' one?"

She looked into his eyes and became weak. "I love my man." She walked away from him struggling in pain with each step that she took.

Three-O laughed under his breath before an evil scowl plastered across his face. "A hundred bricks my nigga, the clock starts now. Tick muthafuckin' tock."

Jimmy Bands waited until the Choppa Gang was out of the door before he roared at the top of his lungs and took off up the stairs to find MayBaby. He located her in the bathroom holding an ice pack to her bruised ribs. She breathed raggedly, looking up at him. He took a step into the hallway and grabbed his .9 millimeter out of the closet and glided into the bathroom once again, he took the gun and pressed the barrel to her forehead. "Open yo' mafuckin' mouth right now bitch and I ain't playing either."

"Why, what did I do?" She stammered about to wet herself.

"Open yo' fuckin' mouth! Do it."

She slowly opened her lips, shaking like a leaf in the wind. "I didn't do anything, baby."

Jimmy Bands stuffed the gun so deep into her throat that he caused her to gag over the barrel. He forced her into the wall and stuffed it further down until she was coughing and gagging loudly. "Bitch, I will kill you. I will blow yo' brains out if you ever choose another nigga over me. I'm it. I'm yo' muthafuckin' god. You get that dumb shit in yo' head to go and fuck off wit' Three-O or anybody else and I swear to the Lord that I will murder from yo mama on down. Do I make myself clear? Huh? Tell me!" He stuffed it some more. She began throwing up all over the barrel. He applied more pressure until he was grunting and jabbing the barrel into her orifice.

MayBaby slapped at his hands purging her guts. Her ribs screamed. Her knees buckled. She fell to the ground crying. "I'll never leave you. I don't have nowhere else to go. I held you down and did everything I was supposed to do. Why are you treating me like this?" She cried.

Jimmy Bands was already in a zone. He grabbed her by the hair after imagining Three-O taking her away from him. He dragged her into the hallway and ripped her clothes off of her within seconds. He forced her thighs apart and entered her hard, placing the gun aside and choking her neck sadistically. "You belong to me, bitch! Me, only! Fuck Crane Creek! Fuck Choppa Gang. This mine! All mine!" He choked her with all of his strength while he stroked her faster and faster. Sweat dripped off of his chin. He licked the side of her face and trembled with power and control.

MayBaby struggled to breathe. Her eyes bugged out of her head. She pried at his fingers to no avail. Next, she was beating at them. He refused to release his hold. Her heart began to pound and skip beats. She grew faint and passed out. Jimmy Bands maintained his assault until he was finished. Then he stood up and came all over her face and breasts. He shook his dick off and stood over her unmoving body. He waited for her to move and when she didn't, he became angry. He balled his fist and punched her as hard as he could in the stomach.

Whoosh!

MayBaby let out a gust of air and screamed rolling on to her side. She curled into a tight ball. "Help me. Help me please." Her eyes crossed and then she went slack.

***

"You see that shit thurr? I told you those Cane Creek niggaz was about to link up with those Duffle Bag boys. Why the fuck would Three-O be over there hollering at Jimmy Bands if they weren't?" Lil Duke asked his brother Big Stupid.

Big Stupid mugged Three-O's car and cocked his Kay. "Say Mane, wait 'til they get to one of those lights, and let's show 'em what dis Grape Street shit all about. Fuck these niggaz. Hurry up, bruh."

Lil Duke stepped on the gas. "Say less big homie, y'all get ready back thurr, we finna chop these niggaz down."

Ghost

Chapter 8

Three-O turned up the Moneybagg, *A Gangster's Pain* album that blared out of his speakers. He nodded his head to the music and tapped his fingers on the steering wheel of his red SRT looking over at his passenger, a trusted Cane Creek shooter he'd personally brought into the game when the youngster was just twelve years old. The young savage nodded his head back at Three-O before turning his vision back out of the window. He was on the hunt for all forms of predators just like he'd been taught by all the big homeys of Cane Creek.

Three-O balled his face and shook his head. "Mane, I don't give a fuck what a nigga gotta say, if it ain't us fuckin' the game up wit' dis music shit den it's Moneybagg. That nigga says da shit my heart be feeling. That's my mafucka right thurr." He looked all around the car until the other four people that were present agreed with him by their subtle head nods. Three-O leaned his seat back a bit and grabbed the bottle of Lean out of the console. He pulled up to the red lights on Ragan Street and halted. He turned the bottle all the way up, downing it greedily as if he was dying of thirst.

Lil Duke opened the side door to the black-on-black stolen Dodge Caravan. He cocked his assault rifle. He had a purple bandana covering his face. He placed the handle up against his shoulder for support and waited until Big Stupid pulled beside Three-O's car before he took aim at Three-O. "Say, bitch niggaz! Y'all plotting on the mob wit dem Duffle Bag niggaz?"

Three-O looked up and his eyes got as big as pool balls. "Aw shit!"

Boom! Boom! Boom! Boom!

The passenger's head exploded right beside Three-O. Brains splashed onto the side of his face and all over the windshield. His shooters started to buss at the van where Lil Duke was shooting from. Glass shattered all around the car. One of Lil Duke's back up shooters caught two to the face and fell out of the van shaking in the middle of the road until his soul left his body.

Three-O stepped on the gas and zipped into traffic with Big Stupid hot on his tail. Two more shooters that were inside of the van began to let their rifles ride rapidly. Three-O's SRT was rocked from side to side. Big holes decorated the candy paint job. Another one of Three-O's lil homies caught a round to the head. He fell forward against the driver's seat with his plasma leaking all over the headrest. Three-O swerved and clipped a Ford 150. The SRT did a three sixty in the middle of the street and emitted smoke from its tires as Three-O brought it to a stop.

Lil Duke jumped out of the van and ran toward the SRT aiming for the driver. His bullets slammed into Three-O's door and cut through it. Three-O felt two slugs eat up his left thigh before they slammed into the dashboard. He hollered out in agony and smashed on the gas with his right foot storming away determined to evade the fire.

Lil Duke ran back to the van and hopped inside of it. "Follow those bitch ass niggaz. I know I hit him. I swear I heard that fuck nigga holler."

Big Stupid backed the van all the way up and wound up on the residential street. "Fuck that lil bruh, don't worry about it. We gon' get they ass. For now, we gotta shake this van cause this ho hot, and den we gotta lay low for a minute."

"But that SRT fucked up, they can't make it that far, all you gotta do is get me kind of close and I'll finish the job. We blast Three-O and Pooh ain't gon' be a problem. Them niggaz do every thang together the whole city know dat." Lil Duke was in kill mode and he couldn't fathom letting Three-O roll away when they were so close to finally murdering him. Grape

Street hated Cane Creek and Choppa Gang. The war had been on for a few summers and as it stood Grape Street were four dead homies down to Choppa Gang, the streets were beginning to refuse to take Grape Street seriously.

"Like I said little brother, we gotta be smart. We'll catch up to his ass again and when we do the set gon' be smoking on that nigga's ashes. That's on every thang. Big Stupid said this with an intense mug plastered across his face.

Lil Duke was frustrated. He put his Kay down on the side of him and punched the door so hard that it left a dent. "Fuck it den bruh, damn! Let's go dump this mafucka then. Ain't no sense of rolling around in it, niggaz ain't tryna to see Shelby County, it's to hot to be in jail."

"I agree, and mark my words, we gon' catch those niggaz lacking. We always do." Big Stupid stepped on the accelerator headed for the murky creek where they would burn the van and push it into the alligator infested waters.

***

Jahliyah two-stepped from side to side and spun in a circle in the big backyard of the mansion. She had a spatula in her left hand, and a pink apron around her neck. The sunlight shone brightly causing her forehead to shine with both sweat and the sheen from her make-up. She flipped the barbecued burgers over and continued to groove to the Summer Walker track; her playlist boomed out of the speakers situated all around the backyard. It was June Nineteenth and the first time that the federal government had recognized the special day as a holiday for Blacks. Taurus made a big deal about wanting to have a nice celebratory meal with the least amount of drama as possible, so Jahliyah volunteered to take upon the task of grilling a few choice meats while Natalia said that she'd take care of the desserts and side dishes. Jahliyah sunk her chef's brush into the pot of special sauce that she'd made and swiped the burgers with it before she added slices of American and Mozzarella cheese. When her playlist flipped over to H.E.R., she closed her eyes for a second and began to sing along with the new track.

Natalia came out of the patio doors at the sounds of Jahliyah's voice. She lowered her Cartier frames and glared at her sister who sang beautifully. A feeling deep within the pit of her stomach came over her. She took the potato salad and sat it on the picnic table beside the twenty-five-meter pool. She looked over at her sister once again and hated how perfect Jahliyah's voice sounded. *Damn, do this bitch do everything right, ugh I hate her.* She sized Jahliyah's burgundy and blue one-piece Burberry swim suit up. The material clung to her body so tightly that it looked like a second skin. Her beautiful caramel tone seemed to glow in the sunlight. Her body was immaculate, and what irritated Natalia the most was the fact that Jahliyah had such a perfect stomach that was full of abs as if she worked on it every single day. She ran her hand over her own stomach that if not for the few faint stretch marks would have been as equally perfect.

Jahliyah opened her eyes and caught her sister watching her. She stopped and stared angrily at her for a moment. They locked eyes. Jahliyah wanted to say something real petty until she remembered the small request of no drama that Taurus had asked of them. You know what, I'm a kill this bitch wit' kindness. She waved Natalia over. "Sis, come here for a second. I want you to taste somethin'.'

Natalia snapped out of her murderous zone. She had been so far gone imagining Jahliyah's death she hadn't even realized that she'd stopped dancing. She straightened up and was caught off guard. "What you say?"

"I said I want you to taste somethin'. Come 'ere." She waved her over again.

Natalia kept her composure and traveled around the gorgeous pool. The ice blue water shimmered. There was a yellow, blue, and red beach ball floating across the small waves, and the scent of chlorine filled the air along with the aroma of the barbecue that Jahliyah was putting down.

Jahliyah took a bratwurst and cut it in half. She dunked it into the sauce and held it up on a fork when Natalia got closer. "Girl, ain't no sense of you being over thurr mugging me, huh, taste dis right thurr."

Natalia stepped back, "no thank you. For all I know yo' ass could be trying to poison me."

Jahliyah laughed, "n'all, I would never do nothing like that, and I know you wouldn't either. I don't hate you because at the end of the day we are still sisters and it's our job to have each other's backs."

"Man," Natalia smacked her lips and grabbed the fork from Jahliyah, eating the sample. She chewed it for a second and then closed her eyes briefly. "Mmm, now that's bomb. I see you know what you're doing. I gotta give you your props on that." She looked over the big pile of meat that Jahliyah had already cooked and became hungry.

Jahliyah already knew what it was before she could ask her. "Don't trip. Before everybody get hurr, I'ma gone and make you a lil' sum-sum." She put together a plate with a Brat, cheeseburger, and two Shish Kabobs. "Here you go."

Natalia took the plate and her stomach growled. "Why are you being so nice to me all of the sudden? Don't act like you don't hate me as much as I hate you."

"I don't hate you. I may be a little jealous of you because of the relationship that you have with our father, but I don't hate you. My mother always said that it's a major sin to hate anybody, and that nobody should get that much of your energy."

"Yeah, well, my mother hated everybody including me at times. And I don't really detest you either. I don't work well with competition. I want our father all to myself because I've been so deprived of him my entire life, solely living off his legacy. When I tracked him down and had him freed, I was sure that it would just be him and I. But then I found out about you and JaMichael, and I instantly became irritated."

"Why would that make you irritated? You should rejoice that you have siblings that could have potentially loved you like no other, I don't get it."

Natalia shrugged, "I don't know. Maybe I don't want that kind of love. Taurus's love is enough for me, his and that of my son, Taurus Jr." She licked the side of the Burger just to get a taste of the barbecue sauce again.

Jahliyah was still trying to figure her out. "Can I ask you an honest question without offending you?" Two Bullies wandered out of the mansion and walked slowly around the pool before settling at Jahliyah's foot. She tossed them two Brats that hadn't been lathered in sauce yet. The two dogs took the meat and ran away with it.

"You can ask me anything, go ahead." Natalia set the plate down and looked into Jahliyah's eyes.

"Did you track our father down so you could be with him in a relationship, or because you were desperately in need of the parent that is him?"

Natalia flared her nostrils. "Why do I feel like you're attacking me right now?"

Jahliyah held up her hands with the spatula still in the left one. "Hey if you don't want to answer it you don't have to. I was just curious."

Natalia ran her fingers through her long curly hair. She looked past Jahliyah's shoulder and saw Taurus sliding the patio daughter all the way open with two big bags in his hands. "Hold that thought, I'll address that later." She turned and jogged away. "Daddeee, what took you so long?" She rushed up to Taurus and hugged his body tightly with her eyes closed once again. The scent of his cologne drove her crazy.

Taurus hugged her back and laughed, "girl, one of these bags have pops in 'em. My arm is already shaky."

Natalia backed up and grabbed the heaviest bag carrying it. She took a hold of his hand and pulled toward the mansion. "Come here I need to ask you a quick question before we all hobnob together. It'll only take a few seconds."

"Well, hold on baby, it smells really good out here. Let me see what my baby girl putting down. Damn, it smells good." Taurus smiled and winked at Jahliyah.

Natalia became flustered. "Hold on Daddy, please. Just come here for one second." She pulled him toward the entrance of the door once again.

Taurus stopped her and was a few seconds away from snapping because of how rude she was being but somehow, he managed to keep his temper in check. He walked into the mansion beside her and closed the patio doors. "Natalia, what is the prob–."

She jumped on him and wrapped her thighs around his body. Before he could say a word, she kissed his lips and slipped her tongue into his mouth.

Taurus allowed her to do this for a moment before he shook her off. She got down slowly and looked up at him in confusion. He took a step back and shook his head. Natalia was lost. She looked at him over quizzically.

"Baby, you gotta take it easy sometimes. You keep forgetting that what we doing ain't normal. I understand you love yo' daddy and all of that but this ain't cool."

Natalia frowned, "what ain't cool? I don't understand?"

"This baby. You can't keep snatching me up and being so obsessive every time you see me. You need to know I ain't going nowhere. Daddy loves you, and I'm right here."

"Well, excuse me for loving my daddy and wanting to express it every time I see him. I didn't see Jahliyah break her neck to get over here to you, but I did, that's why you should love me more than everybody else. Do you, daddy?" She came to him and looked into his honey brown eyes with her baby blues.

Taurus took a hold of the side of her face and melted. "You're my world baby. I know you're simply starving for love and affection, and that you've been looking for me your entire life and now that you have me you don't want to lose me. I get that, and I will never leave nor forsake you, but honestly we have to establish a healthier relationship because this one ain't it."

Natalia shrugged, "it is for me. I don't care how other girls want to be loved by their daddies, this is how I want to be loved by you and I ain't accepting no less than this form. The world can kiss my ass. I love my daddy and we get real nasty together behind closed doors. I love it!" She jumped up and kissed his lips before hugging him tightly. "I'm sorry I'm so crazy about you Daddy, I just can't help it. You're everything."

Taurus held her and sighed, "you are too, lil' Boo Boo."

Jahliyah stuck her head inside of the patio doors and cleared her throat. "Uh, I don't mean to break things up between the two of you, but the food is ready and I'm starving."

"Then go eat then." Natalia rolled her eyes.

Jahliyah smacked her lips, "Daddy, you said no drama today. Can you please talk to your yellow ass daughter because she's about to get on my last nerve?"

Taurus groaned, and rubbed his temples as Natalia hugged him tighter, "y'all gon drive me absolutely crazy, I already see where this is about to go."

"That ain't me, it's her." Jahliyah retorted, glaring at Natalia.

Natalia stuck her tongue out. "Whatever, maybe we ain't hungry for your nasty barbecue."

"Cool den," Jahliyah walked away, closing the patio doors behind her.

Taurus released Natalia, "that wasn't nice, baby. That's not okay." He left Natalia standing there while he pursued Jahliyah.

"Father in heaven, I don't think they truly understand that I killed my own mother for what I wanted. Lord, I know I begged for forgiveness after I did that and I feel like you forgave me, but if I took my sister out of the game, how would you handle me? Please, send me a sign because this broad has got to go."

Ghost

Chapter 9

"Phoenix, why are you always spoiling me? I don't thank even if my Daddy was alive that he would be doing all of this for me like you are?" Cassie asked while stuffing ten bags full of designer clothing into the back seat of Phoenix's black Porsche 718 Boxster Cayman. After she was situated, she pulled suicide doors down and her seat belt came around her slim, thick frame. She was caramel with naturally curly hair, a gorgeous face, and a figure that caused men to do a double take even though she was only seventeen years old. Her steady comparison was that of Meagan Good.

Phoenix was next to pull his door down. He placed his bottle of Lean in the console after taking a long drank and popping two Percocets chewing them and swallowing. He hit the bottle of codeine again and smiled at her, his grill was flooded with thirty-two diamond teeth. His lap was filled with a bag full of cash that he had placed inside of a Crown Royal bag. "Shawty, you already know what it is. I told yo' ass I had you ever since the first day I found out you were my uncle Juice's lil' girl. I can't have you trapping through Memphis looking all ratchet and shit. You feel me?"

She crossed her thighs and applied more gloss to her juicy lips. "Yeah, I feel you. I'm glad somebody tryna be stand up in our family. Ever since I was a little girl, nobody ever did anything for me or my mama, and that's sad because all I hear about in these streets is Taurus and my daddy. That gets annoying."

Phoenix felt a way. He hated whenever he tried to do something in the streets his name was always overshadowed by that of Taurus. He decided once and for all that it was on his shoulders to put his uncle in the dirt. The only way for a legend to be killed was by a legend killer, and Phoenix felt deep within his heart that he was exactly that. "Anyway shawty, yo' moms ain't gotta worry about you no more. I'ma hold you down. Ain't no more living in the projects on Grape Street. You rockin' wit' yo' big cousin, and I'ma spoil yo' ass. You cool wit' that?" He punched the accelerator causing the Porsche to roar like a vicious lion.

"I don't know; my mama is really overprotective. I ain't never spent a night away from the house, and for as long as I've been alive, she ain't never been nothing less than overprotective of me. I thank you gon' have a hard time getting me out of her hands."

Phoenix zipped through the parking lot of the shopping mall until he sped out onto the busy street sending smoke up behind his Porsche. The pipes sang loudly. "Say shawty, I already know how yo' mama gets down. She one of those old Holy Rollers that thank everybody outside of the church is the devil. I ain't trippin' 'bout how difficult she gon' make thangs, just as long as you know that when it's all said and done, yo' lil' ass gon' be wit' me more than you thank. You'll see." He eyed her well-oiled thighs.

"Yeah, well, dis is about to be quite interesting. All I can say is that I'm thankful you care about me enough to be doing all dis. I still can't believe she allowed me to go wit' you for the weekend. I don't know what kind of hold you got over my mama but you're the first."

Phoenix smiled, money ran the world, and a slick nigga's conversation ran the nation. When it came to finessing Charlotte for Cassie it was no different. Unbeknownst to Cassie, her mother was struggling financially, and had fallen into hard times. A man had broken Charlotte's heart but not before turning her on to the Rebirth. Now that Charlotte was hooked Phoenix saw a way to pry Cassie loose. He had plans for her. Natalia was vastly becoming old news.

"So, what are we about to do in Arkansas for the weekend? Ain't it nuthin' but country folk over dat way?"

Phoenix nodded, "but it ain't about them, it's about me getting to know my lil cousin after a few years. You're almost a young woman. We have a lot of catching up to do." He grabbed a stack of cash from between his legs. "Huh you don't worry about nothin' just sit back and count this money, this what I plan on spending on you this weekend just to make up for some of the lost time between us."

"Dang cuz, I thank I love you already." Cassie leaned over and kissed him on the cheek before she started to count the twenty thousand dollars that he'd placed in her lap. Finally, there was somebody outside of her mother that cared for her.

***

Knock. Knock. Knock.

Jahliyah read another sentence of Jelissa's novel, *Love Me Even When It Hurts*, before she sat the book down and perked up. "Who is it?"

"It's me, lil' baby. What are you doing?" Taurus asked. Jahliyah had spent the last two days locked inside of her room reading Jelissa's entire book collection. Out of all the authors in the game, Jelissa was her favorite because of the emotional, page turning journey, amongst so many other things, she took her readers on every time. "I'm just chilling, Daddy. I'm at peace. What's going on?"

Taurus tried the doorknob and found it locked. "Baby, open the door. I need to holler at you for a minute."

Jahliyah remained seated for a few seconds, sighed, and got up. She opened the door and stood back allowing him to pass by. "What's up?"

Taurus closed the door behind him and took a hold of her, brushing a strand of curls off her forehead. "You've been in this room for the last two days. I ain't seen you, and I've been worried about you. What's going on?"

Jahliyah shrugged. "I don't know. I guess I'm just tired of all the drama that comes along with being here. Every time I come out and want to spend a little time with you, me and my sister wind up getting into it for nothing. I think I'ma fly back to New York at the end of the week just to get a jump start on a few business decks I need to present to a few key investors. I need to use this time wisely rather than squander it."

Taurus rubbed the side of her soft cheek. "So, you honestly feel like you're squandering your time by being here with me?"

She nodded, "I honestly do. I'm a grown ass woman. There is no way that I should be arguing and almost ready to kill another woman over my own father, especially when she is supposed to be my sister. There are just certain things that I don't get, and I guess I never will." She walked away from him and sat on the bed.

Taurus stood watching her for a moment. She wore a blue and white onesie that had the words Taurus and the zodiac bull sign all over it. Her birthday was only a few days after his, they were both Tauruses on of the many reasons why her birth had meant so much to him. Taurus slipped beside her on the bed and placed his arm around her shoulder. "You're my heart Jahliyah. You're the first child that I ever knew that I had. You were the first person in this world besides my mother that I knew I honestly loved enough to give my life. I'm crazy about you, and I'm not ready for you to go back to New York."

Jahliyah looked up at him. "If all of this is true, Daddy, why do you allow her to get her way all the damn time? Is it because she's lighter than me? You think she is prettier than I am because she's mixed?"

Taurus frowned, "what, baby hell n'all. That doesn't mean anything to me. I'm not one of those dudes that only date and impregnate white or Spanish women just so I can have a so-called gorgeous child. I think you are the most perfect. You are so beautiful in every single way. I am more than proud to be your father. Please, don't get it twisted."

"It's not how I feel. I feel like I'm second best, and as if my thoughts and feelings don't matter when it comes to you. This entire time that I've been here this is the first time that you've actually taken the time out to ask me how I'm doing, and to see what's the matter with me. I don't feel loved here, I feel like a burden and I'm tired of it. I wish I never came." Her throat began to crack up. She cleared it and wiped her eyes before the tears were able to fall down her cheeks.

Taurus caught a lump in his throat, "damn, Boo Boo, I'm so sorry. I didn't know you were feeling like that." He pulled her to him until she was sitting on his lap, then he wrapped his big arms around her. He kissed her forehead. "Jahliyah, I love you with all that I am as a man. You bring me so much joy, and I am so sorry for not being there up until this point. Your father had a crazy life, and even still that's no excuse. I know that I can't change the past, but I would love to try to secure our relationship for the present and future because you mean that much to me, all I ask is that you give me a chance, please baby."

"I don't know because I honestly feel like I've given you more chances than you deserve. I flew all the way here from New York, placing my career and my life on hold just so I could come here and get to know you. But it's like I said, ever since I've been here, I've felt so unwanted, yet I'm still here. When will we be able to spend some alone time together where I can pick your brain? I have so many questions, and so many things that I need to know about my past, my mom, and your history. I am hungry for it."

"Whenever you want, baby. We can shut down for the next couple of days, just you and me so we can get to know each other the right way. I am perfectly cool with that."

Jahliyah smiled weakly, "yeah but what about Natalia? You already know she be all over you. I don't think that she's going to allow you to get a peace of mind for one second away from her. So what are you going to do about that?"

"You don't worry about Natalia. I'll handle her. All I want you to do is to get prepared to leave. There is a nice lil' place just west of Memphis that your father goes too whenever he needs to thank just a bit. I wanna take you there for a few days so that it can solely be about us. Pack yo thangs, we're leaving tonight." He kissed her forehead and kept his lips pressed to it for a bit before he patted her on the butt so that she could get up. He stood over her. "I really love you Jahliyah. I can't have you moping around here feeling like you're not as special as the next person when I love you just as much. We're all a family at the end of the day. That's what it's all about. Get ready, we leave in two hours."

Chapter 10

"Just cause a nigga check dem big bags of gwop in the streets don't mean that a mafucka gotta stop getting down wit' this stick play my nigga, never forget that." Pooh said as he turned into the long dark alley behind Grape Street. A family of raccoons were ravishing through the garbage cans. It smelled like death. A Pit Bull lay in the middle of it dead with maggots crawling all over its flesh and huge rats eating away at its carcass.

Rondo pinched his nose. "It stank like a mafucka over hurr, shawty. What the fuck dat smell is?" He popped his hoodie over his head and cocked his automatic shotgun wanting to roll up his window from the sheer stench of it all.

Three-O laughed in the back seat of the big Bronco. "Dat thurr is the smell of death, baby. It is what it is, ain't shit you can really get around. I'ma take it as a sign that all of these young niggaz that we're about to lay down really had it coming all in the name of war and murder." He downed his whole bottle of codeine and tossed the bottle out of the window of the truck.

"Worse thang a mafucka could ever do was to cross Cane Creek. This Choppa Gang shit ain't to be taken lightly, bitchez cross us and they gotta suffer the consequences, that's just what that is right thurr."

"Yeah Rondo, yo' bitch ass better take notes, cause once you slimed in with the gang any false moves and we gotta have yo head on a platter, I'm talking heinous shit." Three-O let it be known.

Rondo turned around and locked eyes with him. "Fuck, you must be thanking I'm new to dis murder shit or somethin'? It's a reason why they were calling me the Kang of Orange Mound at eighteen-years-old, nigga. It's 'cause I paint shit. My belt is full of more than holes, bitch, I got bodies. Yo' Pooh, what the fuck up wit' Slime back thurr?"

Three-O scoffed, cocking his F&N's one at a time. "On the guys, if Pooh wasn't yo' brother I'd knock yo' head off and serve your brain to my Dobermans. I don't like you, lil' nigga. I hate all you bitchez from the south end of Memphis, including you. Keep dat shit in mind."

"Yeah bitch, well, I don't like you either. I can't trust you. How the fuck you gon' stay solid wit' Choppa Gang but word on the street is you're locked with those Bread Gang niggaz, too? Cane Creek nor Orange Mound don't fuck wit' those opps, explain dat shit?"

"Say niggaz, y'all shut that dumb shit up and get focused. We on a muthafuckin' mission." Pooh snapped. He turned to Rondo, "the homey on strict bidness wit' the Bread Gang. He still slimed into the Choppa Gang as the second seat under me. Never question my nigga's loyalty to the set. You understand that?"

Rondo waved him off, "bitch, I do what I want. I'm Shiesty Gang to the death of me, and I ain't switching sides. I'ma get money wit' my niggaz and my niggas only, fuck the world after that. Fuck him and Bagg, that's on the guys."

Three-O placed both of his weapons to the back of Rondo's head. "Say Pooh, I'm all the brother you need. Let me slump this fuck nigga on some real shit. Got my nigga Bagg in his mouth and all that. Bitch needs some discipline."

Rondo closed his eyes and clenched his jaw in anger. "Yo', take those bitch ass poles from my dome, nigga, or pull the fuckin' trigger wit' yo' bitch ass. Fuck you and Bagg, I ain't stuttering."

"Mane, what the fuck I say? Both you niggaz cut that shit out. Y'all wearing on my patience really bad right now." Pooh snapped.

Three-O removed the guns. "I was just playing. I ain't gon' kill his bitch ass likc that. Just mind yo' mouth, boy or I just might." He tucked his guns and opened the back door after sliding his black mask over his face.

"What the fuck you need that mask for?" Pooh asked cocking his Glock .40s.

"Better safe than sorry my nigga, why you ain't masking up?" Three-O slipped his latex gloves over his hands before applying gloves.

"Ain't no since putting on somethin' that ain't gon' is necessary. Every muthafucka in that house 'bout to go to sleep and ain't a mafuckin' alarm clock on this side of Tennessee gon' be able to wake em' back up, trust and believe dat. Now, let's move."

***

Big Stupid sat down at the kitchen table in front of a big plate of southern fried chicken, collard greens, baked macaroni and cheese, cornbread, and a cherry cheesecake. He tucked a bib into his shirt and looked over all his food, hungrier than he was before he laid eyes on it. "Damn Shanay, you got dis shit looking good as a muthafucka. I hope it tastes just as swell."

Shanay rolled her eyes, "stop playin' wit' me, you already know how I get down. I've been feeding yo' big ol' ass ever since we were in the ninth grade and my mama kicked me out after I got pregnant wit' yo' first big headed kid. Just give me my props when props are due." She sat across from him and started to feed their thirteen-month-old son first, their five-year-old was already chowing down on his food.

Big Stupid sat there for a minute as everybody started to eat but him. He appraised his meal again and suddenly became very thankful. He sniffed it and smiled. "Damn."

"Somethin' wrong wit' yo' meal, baby?" Shanay asked this after wiping some food from the corners of her youngest son's mouth.

"I don't know. I feel like we gotta start praying before we eat or something."

"Praying?" Shanay wanted to make sure that she heard him correctly. "Dat what you said?"

"Yeah, I thank giving a lil' grace to God before we eat ain't too much to ask. What, you don't thank we should or somethin'?"

Shanay shrugged, "I don't know. It's just that we've been together all this time and I ain't never heard you say nuthin' 'bout no praying, finding it odd is all. Ain't gon' bother me one way or the other though."

"Yeah, well, starting tomorrow, whenever we sit our black asses down to eat, we gon' pray, I gotta get my household in order. That's how I feel."

Shanay cheesed, "ooo baby, I like hearing you getting all religious and thangs, make me feel all warm and tingly down south. I feel like it's what we've been missing. Dis one right hurr only five and done took to cussing every chance he got. Just 'bout wanna knock his teeth down his throat next time I catch him doing it."

Big Stupid eyed his son who lowered his head and stuffed a piece of chicken into his mouth. "I'm sorrwee, mama."

"Yeah, I just bet, yo' butt gon' be sorry if dat teacher calls me again saying the worst bout you, now thank it's a game you here?" Shanay snapped.

"Yes ma'am." He returned.

Big Stupid shook his head as the baby spit up his food. Shanay jumped up to attend to the child. The back door was kicked in at the same time. The front door flew off the hinges. Big Stupid stood up in a panic. He reached on his hip for a gun that wasn't there. Shanay screamed at the top of her lungs and grabbed the baby from his highchair.

Three-O slipped into the kitchen from the back door, aimed and fired three times. His bullets slammed into Big Stupid's chest knocking him off his feet and into the refrigerator. Pooh was next to shoot. He popped Shanay in the back of the head causing her to fall to her knees holding her child. She tried as best she could to tuck the baby under her. Pooh kicked her in the ribs and aimed downward, firing his gun over and over murdering both the mother and her child. He emptied the rest of his clip into Big Stupid's face shredding it. Blood filled the kitchen.

The five-year-old jumped off his chair and took off running out of the back door. Three-O fired at him multiple times knocking chunks of wood out of the wall along the door frame. Pooh tried to fire and forgot that he was out of bullets. Rondo turned to chase after the little boy. By the time he got outside, the little boy was already in the alley. Rondo stopped and aimed. His red beam landed on the back of the little boy's head. He took a deep breath and placed his finger over the trigger ready to fire but something in him wouldn't allow him to do it. He fired in the air three times and stood there as the little boy kept running down the alley.

"Say Mane, who da fuck over thurr shooting by cuz 'nem tip. I thank it's a hit!" Came a Grape Street Shooter from across the alley. He waved for his homies to follow him to see what all of the chaos was about.

Rondo rushed back into the house, when he got there Three-O had ripped Shanay's shirt open and was ogling her titties. He licked his lips. "I always wanted to know what this bitch body looked like under these clothes ever since high school, I just had to see." He pulled her skirt up and ripped her panties off, after seeing her privates he stood up nodding. "Yeah, that bitch was bad."

Pooh laughed and grabbed a piece of chicken off Big Stupid's plate, it had specks of blood on it. He tore the meat from the bone with his teeth and smacked loudly. "Damn this shit good."

"Aw, hell n'all!" The same Grape Street Shooter from the alley caught sight of the massacre and nearly flipped his wig. He upped his gun and started firing at Pooh. "Bitch ass nigga!"

Rondo got down on one knee shooting back. His slugs caught the Shooter four to the neck ripping his neck from his shoulder. He fell down the stairs. Rondo chased his body to make sure that he was dead. When he got to the open door headed into the backyard, he saw twenty Grape Street assassins headed by Lil Duke running across the alley. He rushed back into the house. "They coming deep as hell, let's go!"

All three men took off out of the front of the house. They loaded into the Bronco just as slug after slug began to eat up the paint. The windows busted loudly. Pooh swerved and stormed down the street leaving their opps in the rearview mirror.

"Now, dats how you slime a mafucka gang, dats how you represent bitch!" Three-O hollered excitedly.

Pooh looked over at Rondo, "bitch, I see you got the drop before that nigga clipped me. That's real nigga shit right thurr."

Rondo nodded, "I did what I was supposed to do. That's just how the game goes. Ain't no biggie."

"Yeah nigga, ain't no mafuckin' biggie. Stop tryna make this shit all lovey dovey and what not." Three-O laughed.

Pooh smirked, "yeah, awright. Good shit though, niggaz. We'll put Lil Duke in ashes for the set real soon, don't even trip."

"At least we got Big Stupid. That bitch nigga is on a shirt now! Damn I'm up there!" He hollered.

Pooh busted up laughing, "Choppa Gang, bitch. Chop, chop, chop, blurrrrd."

"Blurrrrd, bitch! Blurrrrrrd!" Three-O returned.

Rondo remained quiet. For him to become the king of Memphis, he knew that it would eventually come down to him getting rid of both men. His heart was too cold to be third fiddle. It was a young man's slums and deep down he didn't feel that either Pooh or Three-O was ever going to honor that fact so it was on him to crush them in honor of Shiesty Gang; when the time was right of course. Until then, he figured he'd simply play his role.

Ghost

Chapter 11

It was a warm and beautiful Friday morning with the sun shining, and a slight westward breeze, when Jahliyah stepped into the log cabin and dropped her Hermes bags in the center of the floor. The aroma of hickory caught her attention along with the sights of the interiors of the cabin. "Wow Daddy, we're about to stay here?" She stepped further into their temporary home that they'd be in for the duration of the weekend.

Taurus snatched up her bags and nodded, "I told you that I wanted us to get away. This place here is what I call my thinking tank. Whenever I need to formulate an impenetrable plot, I come here to clear my mind. I hope you love it."

"Do I?" She ran all around the cabin, hopping over the huge brown bear rug that was in the center of the room. She ran her hand along the black leather four-piece living room set and the length of the projector used to watch movies and sports. She squatted down in front of the fireplace. "Daddy, I know it's hot outside and all, but you thank we could possibly light a fire in here? I ain't never chilled in front of one of these before."

"Baby, it's your world. We can do whatever you wanna do because these next few days are all about you." He situated her bags inside of the guest room and came back to find her hugging herself looking up at the painted picture of Princess. She squinted hard and sighed. "Daddy, what was she like?"

Taurus came behind her and wrapped his arms around her waist. "She was a strong, intelligent, jazzy woman. Your mother had heart. She didn't bow down to anybody; not even me and she was a petite woman, too. I don't thank she was more than five-feet-four inches tall and less than a hundred and thirty pounds, but her name rang bells and set off sirens in the streets. Not only was she the love of my life, but she was my right-hand man; the only person in this world I fully trusted."

Jahliyah placed her hands on top of his while she looked up at her mother's eyes. She leaned back into him and closed her eyes. "Am I anythang like her?"

"Yeah baby, you are your mother's twin. I mean, you got just a bit more weight on you, but not much. Other than that, you two are identical."

"N'all, I know I'm the perfect blend of you two, but I guess I'm wondering if I'm more of a push over than she was? Do I possess the same lioness qualities within me as she did, is what I'm asking?"

"I believe you do. I don't think your mother became a fighter, or even stood up for herself until both her and I fell in love. When that happened, we became so much like one another that it was F the world. I brought the animal out of her, just like she brought the savage out of me."

"Guess it's safe to say that you still love her huh, like you kinda wish she was still here and all dat?"

"Most definitely. Princess will always be the love of my life."

Jahliyah smiled, "man, I sho' wish one day I can find a man who'll love me the way you loved her. I've read some thangs in my mother's diary. She definitely said you were the real deal. She didn't play about you, and you didn't play 'bout her either. That's the kind of love that a girl can only read about in an old diary or see in a movie. It just don't exist anymore and that's so sad." Her shoulders slumped.

Taurus picked her back up and rested his lips on her jawline. He kissed her. "You're my lil' baby. *I* love you like that. In my heart and mind, you were my first born. I can still remember the first day I held you in my arms; it was one of the happiest days of my life."

"Aw Daddy, you mean that?"

"I do, and it would have killed me if you would have gone back to New York. I ain't ready to be without my baby girl." He kissed her neck and held her tighter.

Jahliyah couldn't deny the warm and fuzzy feeling his lips gave her. She tried as hard as she could to think of healthy thoughts. She didn't want to envision Taurus in the wrong light. He was her father, and the last parent she had alive on earth. "Daddy, what happened to my mother? For so long, I believed that you...well, you know."

Taurus released her and turned her around, so she was facing him. "Baby, your grandmother, my mother, was not a well woman. My father, your grandfather, was a very abusive man. He was hard on everyone inside of our home, especially your grandmother. Because she was mixed with Black, Creole, and Native American, she was a very beautiful woman, and it made my father very insecure. Long story short, during the times my father beat and humiliated her on a daily basis, I took upon the role as her savior and left the son title behind.

Before either of us could understand what was going on, our relationship developed into something neither of us was prepared for. She became dependent on me and extremely possessive. When Princess and Blaze came into the picture, she never accepted their places in my life. One day, she snapped and killed both. Unfortunately, she told the authorities that I did it. It's crazy, but the story is real. There are movies and books about our family's bloodline and specifically my legendary story, *Raised As A Goon*. I mean, you should already know this. Have you read any of the books?

Jahliyah nodded, "I've read all five of those books and they are juicy, and oh so vivid. But are they true stories?"

"One hundred percent. These books were written by me while I was locked down in the Feds, and I allowed your brother to perfect them. He published them before I could give him the go ahead, but that's another story." He rubbed her face and looked into her eyes. "I love you, Jahliyah and there is nothing in this world I wouldn't do for you. Do you understand that?"

Jahliyah nodded, "yes, I do." She was quiet for a second, then she summoned the nerve to ask him the very thought that'd been plaguing her mind ever since she found out about him and Natalia. "Daddy, I need to ask you somethin'. I'm tryin' to make sense of some things."

"What's on your mind?"

"Natalia; I want to know how you two started sleeping together? Don't tell me you haven't because I've listened and peeked in on the two of you a few times. So, how did it start?"

Taurus's eyes drifted off. "Damn, you came ready for action today, huh?"

She nodded, "I just want to know."

Taurus pulled her over to the couch and allowed her to sit on his lap sideways. He lowered his head for a second and took a deep breath. "To be honest, baby. I don't know."

"Come on now. You're going to have to come a little harder than that."

He exhaled, "I'm not perfect. Our blood is filthy, baby. Connecting emotionally for me always seems to lead to sex, ultimately creating a dangerous bond. With Natalia, it just happened from one intimate moment. The next thing I knew we were going there. I'm not proud of myself and I know I should've had more discipline than that because she's my daughter, but I didn't. Because of that, I am sure we will never have a normal relationship again."

"Did you enjoy her?"

"What kind of question is that? I don't thank I know how to answer that."

"No; what I mean is what goes through your mind when you're having sex with your *own* blood, your child?"

"Damn, you making this hard." Taurus began to perspire. "I don't know. I guess the same thing that goes through your mind when you're having sex with somebody but without that taboo feeling and the excitement that comes along with knowing you aren't supposed to be doing what you're doing. That's the best way I can answer that, Boo Boo."

Jahliyah adjusted herself on his lap until one thick thigh was on each side of him. She held his shoulders and looked into his eyes. "Why her, though, Daddy? You have two of us. Why did you choose her over me? Is it because she's prettier?"

Taurus hated himself for feeling a way. The weight of Jahliyah in his lap was causing his manhood to harden. It didn't help that her skirt had risen and was now at her waist. The scent of her perfume wafted up his nostrils. He felt her adjust until she was sitting on the length of him. His penis started throbbing and jumping up against her heat. She cocked her back and humped forward ever so slightly. He didn't know if it was intentional or accidental.

"Baby, I saw you come out of the womb. I loved your mother with all that I was as a man. I know that she is my biological daughter, too, but for some reason it felt as if you are more of my daughter than she was. I never saw you in that sexual light and with her, for some reason, I did."

Jahliyah winced, "damn, I don't know what to take from that." She pressed her forehead against his. "Do you love me?"

"Yea Boo, I do. I love you with all of my heart."

She leaned down until her lips were brushing his. "Am I your baby Daddy, huh, are you crazy about your baby girl?"

Taurus began to shake, "one hunnit percent."

Jahliyah pressed her juicy lips against his and dropped her weight into his lap. She felt the length of him throbbing against her panty crotch all the way unto the piece of material that split her cheeks. Her thick thighs spread a bit. "I'm crazy about my Daddy too. You thank she the only one wit' yo blood inside of her? Well, she ain't." She licked his lips and turned all the way around until her back was against his chest. She held his knees and slowly rocked back and forth giving him a subtle lap dance. Her knees were spaced as far apart as she could get them.

Taurus moaned, and sucked on the back of her neck. He took his big hands and slid them into the neckline of her blouse taking a hold of her B cups. Her hard nipples poked up against the palms of his hands. He pulled her shirt up to free her breasts. "Damn baby, what are you doing to me?"

"Nothing." She lifted and squeezed his big dick. She stroked it and sat back in his lap. Now his piece was throbbing like crazy. She repeated the same process again and sat back. She pulled her panties to the side and twerked in his lap.

"Uh, fuck, Jahliyah. Baby, please don't do this." He was struggling to control himself.

"What, Daddy? We ain't doing nothing. I'm just dancing in *my* daddy's lap. Ain't nothing wrong with that, is it?"

Taurus moaned louder. He lifted her up and pulled his dick out of his pants and lowered her back down. Now it was flesh on flesh. Jahliyah groaned at the feel of his hot skin. Her twerking persisted. Taurus's dick sawed in and out of her pussy lips without penetrating her. In a matter of minutes, his entire lap was soaking wet with her juices.

Taurus beat on the arm of the sofa in torture. He lifted her up once again and this time slowly slid his dick head inside of her hot tight pussy. Jahliyah moaned and stood up. She wagged her finger at him. "No Daddy, no sex. We can't do that. It's forbidden."

Taurus was shaking so bad. Before he knew what he was doing, he had her bent over the couch with his face in her crack licking up and down her crease hungrily. Taurus would trap them and suck all over them loudly before he located her clitoris licking circles around it. Jahliyah moaned at the top of her lungs and acted as if she was trying to swat him away. Taurus kept eating until she screamed and came all over his face, then he turned her around again and stuffed her knees to her chest. From this position he was able to devour her pussy while she shook and came back-to-back screaming about how much she loved him. Taurus's chin dripped with her secretions. He squeezed his own dick, stroking it, yearning to put it inside of Jahliyah.

Jahliyah came for the fourth time and kicked out of his hold. She stood up on shaky knees with her cum running down her thick thighs. Her fingers rubbed her bald pussy. Both nipples were standing up on her chest like two pencil erasers. "We can't go further, Daddy. We just can't."

Taurus nodded from the couch. He knew if he stood, he would wind up taking the pussy. He wanted her so bad. Instead, he pulled her to him by her backside and kissed her gap again. His tongue eased inside of her lips over and over.

Jahliyah placed her foot on the couch and took a hold of his head humping with her eyes closed. "Daddy. Daddy. Mmm, I'm supposed to be your baby. You're not supposed to be doing this. Aww, shit you not." She felt him flick her clit and slurp it into his mouth loudly, making her scream.

She pushed Taurus away and fell to the carpet convulsing as a massive orgasm rocked her body. Taurus stood over her with his dick swinging from side to side. He wiped the juices from his mouth. "Damn, I gotta go take a cold shower. I gotta calm down. If I don't I'ma wind up tearing dat ass up." He hurried away to do just what he said.

Jahliyah made her way to her feet. Her chest heaved up and down. "Yeah Daddy, you do that. I'ma get in right after you." She placed her arms back into the loopholes of her blouse, fixed her panties back over her mound and pulled her skirt down.

A trail of juice slid down her inner thigh all the way to her ankles. She wiped it up with her hand and sucked her fingers. "Damn, there's something wrong with me." The shower sounded upstairs while there was a knock on the door. The sudden noise scared Jahliyah half to death. She took a moment to gather herself, walked over and opened the door. As soon as she saw the person standing in front of it, her heart sank into the deepest recesses of her stomach.

Chapter 12

"Oh my God, girl, damn, what are you doing here?" Jahliyah asked, irritated.

Natalia stepped past her, "I ain't gotta answer that question, you ain't nobody to me. I miss my Daddy, and I came to see him. Where is he at?" She scanned the living room and eventually her eyes led over to the stairs to see if she could locate him.

Jahliyah closed the door. "Girl, I don't mean to be rude and all that but damn, you are a bug-a-boo. You act like you gotta be up his ass all the time. What's the matter with allowing me to spend a little alone time with him before I go back to New York?"

"Because; why do you have to be alone with him? Why can't we all spend some time together? I mean, he's just coming back into my life, too. What makes you so special?"

"Natalia, when I first got here you were coming off a two-week vacation where it was just you and him. I waited patiently back at the mansion and kept my comments to myself. You mean to tell me you can't give me two days alone with *our* father? That ain't right nor is it fair."

"Jahliyah, life isn't fair. And if I leave you two alone together, who's to say that by the time he gets back to the mansion he won't love you more than me? After all, I'm only his biracial daughter from a woman he never gave two fucks about, whereas with you, he was in love with your mother, and you look so much like her. I can only imagine what goes through his mind when it comes to you."

"Damn, Natalia. Why does it have to be a competition between the two of us? I can't compete with you. You're rich, you're strong, you got our father out of prison and you're absolutely stunning. There is no comparison."

Natalia was silent for a minute. She ran her fingers through her naturally long curly hair, "do you honestly mean that?"

"Yeah, I do. I know I could never compete with you, and I'd never try. Look, I'm heading back to New York as soon as this weekend is over. Daddy knows that, and now you know. All I'm asking is for these last two days. It's not even two because we're leaving first thing Sunday morning. Come on, I ain't asking for much."

Natalia took a deep breath and exhaled loudly. "But I already drove all the way here."

"Come on sis, please? I would owe you big. Anything you want."

"For you to go away and to never return, if I'm being quite honest. If I do this, I don't want you sleeping with our father. That's mine and his bond only. That's our special thing. I don't care about an emotional connection, hugs and all of that, but that's it. Can you promise me that?"

"For sure." *Who the fuck do this bitch think she is,* Jahliyah wondered? "That's not even something that has ever crossed my mind, his neither. We are strictly father and daughter; I promise you that."

Natalia read her eyes and saw sincerity. "Fuck, okay den, Jahliyah but y'all better be back first thing Sunday morning and no later, or I will get even in a way you will never see coming. I don't play about my Daddy. Don't make me show you who I really am. You got that?"

Bitch, fuck you. "Yeah, I got it, sis. You don't have anything to worry about." She crossed her finger over her heart.

Natalia pointed at her. "Awright den." She picked up her bags and headed back out the door but not before turning back around to look into Jahliyah's eyes.

Jahliyah waited until Natalia's Bentley truck was halfway down the long road that led up to the cabin before she pulled her blouse over her head and slipped out of her skirt. She took the stairs one at a time and opened the bathroom door.

Taurus stood with his eyes closed pumping his piece with forbidden thoughts of Jahliyah plaguing his mind. He groaned ever so slightly. He squeezed his eyelids tighter. When the shower curtains were pulled back, he froze and opened them.

Jahliyah stepped into the shower and adjusted the temperature. "Daddy, I'm right here. You ain't gotta do none of that no more." She turned around with her back to him. His hard dick went right between her ass cheeks forcing it further into her crack.

"What are you doing, Boo Boo?"

Jahliyah backed up and rubbed her booty all over his hard dick that started to elongate the more it touched her delicate skin. "We ain't doing nothing wrong if you don't go inside of me, right?" She took a hold of his dick and rubbed the crabapple sized head all over her pussy mound that was shielded by her panties. She pressed it on the opening, but the cloth prevented him from sliding inside of her.

Taurus groaned and took a hold of her hips. This was his first time really realizing just how thick she was. "Baby, you're driving me crazy right now. You gotta get out or we're finna cross that line."

"No, we ain't, Daddy, trust me, I got this." She pulled the panties all the way to the side to reveal her meaty pussy. The water from the shower rained down on it causing it to glisten. She spread the lips with two fingers exposing her pink to him. "Look at this juicy pussy, Daddy. I know you want this pussy." She took a hold of his dick and rubbed it up and down between her sex lips. The feel of his flesh against hers made her weak. She sucked on her bottom lip and shivered.

Taurus darted his hips forward and slid in two inches. Her heat seared him. She was too hot and too tight. Her juices began to leak out of her. "Baby girl, fuck, what are you doing?"

Jahliyah moaned as he slid a few more inches inside of her. She leaned forward and pulled him out. "No Daddy, I'm your baby." She turned around to face him. She kissed his lips and ran his head in between her bald labia. She humped forward over and over.

Taurus pushed her back to the shower wall and kissed her lips hard. He licked along her neck and bit her. His hand went in between her legs, cuffed her pussy, spread it, and slipped two fingers deep into her. "You're my baby girl. All mine!"

Jahliyah placed her foot on the edge of the tub. Taurus finger-fucked her at full speed while they sucked all over each other's tongues. She moaned into his mouth and bucked against him. Taurus groaned just as much, squeezing her juicy booty and licking all over her neck and shoulder blades, when he ventured down and started to suck her gum drop nipples Jahliyah screamed and came all over his fingers. She couldn't help it. Taurus had been stroking her G spot for ten minutes straight, finding it amusing that she got off just as quick like her mother.

He pulled his fingers out and cleaned them with his mouth. "Damn Jahliyah, we gotta stop. Daddy so fuckin' hard lil' baby, but we gotta stop."

Jahliyah agreed. She grabbed the loofah and lathered the both of them up. They showered and got out. Jahliyah walked out of the bathroom with her ass jiggling and her titties bouncing on her slim-thick frame. When she stepped into the bedroom to get a change of underwear, Taurus came up behind her and pushed her over it. He dropped down and stuffed his face into her crevices again. This time he took all of twenty minutes to make her cum back-to-back. He threw her knees over his shoulders and ate her for another ten minutes before she passed out with him sucking each of her toes.

When she woke up, Taurus had her laid on his chest cuffing her booty cuffed with his big hands. She stirred and they locked eyes. Jahliyah sat up and straddled him. She laid her head on his shoulder again. "Daddy, are you mad at me?"

Taurus held her by her ass and kissed her lips. "Why would I be mad at you, baby?"

"Because I'm sure it seems like I'm just teasing you, but that's not my intention. I mean I wanna go there with you, every part of me does but I know it's wrong no matter how much I really want you."

"Well, I'm not mad at you. What type of man would I be?" He kissed her lips again and rubbed all over her booty, squeezing it. "I love you too much to ever be mad at you."

Jahliyah leaned down and placed her forehead to his. "How much do you want me though?"

Taurus tensed. She was driving him crazy. "I don't know how to answer that question."

"With honesty; that's how you're always supposed to answer anything when it comes to us. So how much?" She bit into his neck and humped into him slowly, yet firmly.

"A-a-a lot. You're driving me crazy." He slid his fingers down to her crack and slipped his middle one into her pussy again.

Jahliyah tilted her head back and moaned, "Daddy, what if you just put it in a little bit. Not all of the way but just enough to get you there. Would that be okay?"

Taurus's dick began to jump crazily. He pulled her down until her box was covering it. "T-t-that's up to you." He stuttered imagining the feeling of her.

Jahliyah scooted upward and took a hold of his dick again and eased the head past her lips with her mouth wide open.

She scratched his lower back and screamed. Taurus plunged deeper and deeper before he growled and pulled out of her pumping his piece. His semen flew all over her stomach and pussy. She hopped to all fours and took a hold of it, sucking it into her mouth moaning all around it as he dumped his seed more and more. She fell to her back breathing heavily.

Taurus laid beside her and pulled her over to him kissing her forehead. "Baby, you good? You sho' you ain't gon' feel a way about what we just did?"

Jahliyah shook her head. "N'all Daddy, or at least I hope not. I don't want to thank 'bout that right now. I just want you to hold me. I feel good and at this moment, that's all that matters." She snuggled up against his chest. She couldn't help but remember the promise she'd made to Natalia about flying back to New York on Sunday. She wasn't so sure if she was willing to stick to that now. She couldn't imagine leaving the city after what her and Taurus had just done.

Taurus felt guilty as he held her. He cursed himself for being so weak. *What the fuck is wrong with me? Why do I keep giving in to his kind of shit, h*e asked himself? He held Jahliyah tighter. "Baby, I know you don't want to talk about any of this shit right now, but I'm sorry, Boo Boo. I love you with all of my heart, and I'm just sorry."

Jahliyah climbed atop him and laid on his chest. "You're good, Daddy. We're good. Just hold me. That's all I ask right now. That's all that matters.

"Okay, baby. I got you." Taurus closed his eyes and kept his big arms wrapped around her small frame until they drifted off to sleep, both snoring lightly.

From three blocks over, a teary-eyed Natalia watched the monitors that had the entire log cabin under surveillance. She balled both of her fists and stomped her right foot. "How could you Daddy? How could you do this to me!" She screamed.

She fell to her knees with her hands covering her face, breaking down worse than she ever had in her entire life. When it was all said and done nothing, but the ultimate revenge consumed her mind. She promised to make the both of them pay.

Chapter 13

"What that nigga on, Slime? He's still on that bitch jacking?" Three-O asked Pooh as they rolled through Crane Creek at five o'clock in the evening sipping Lean and tooting lines of the Rebirth.

Pooh adjusted the Draco on his lap and nodded his head. "Yeah mane, Lil Duke bitch ass been on this mafucka capping about the set for over thirty minutes. I'm trying to make out where the fuck he streaming this video from. I got a couple hoez chiming in trying to get him to drop his location. When he drops that bitch, we gon' roll through there and put his monka ass on a shirt."

Three-O laughed. "As we do so well. How many pints of Grape Street we sippin' on so far, I know you keep track of that kind of shit?"

"We up five pints now after we dropped Big Stupid and his family. Them niggaz should be hollering that truce shit instead of having this goofy ass nigga on social media doing all of this dumb shit. Seems like a mafucka doesn't learn unless you wipe out they whole click." Pooh said before he took a long swallow from his Codeine infested drink.

"Den dats what we gon' have to do den. Dat shit don't make me no never mind." Three-O nodded out for a brief second, but before his head could hit the steering wheel, he snapped back awake. He ran his hand over his face and sat up.

Pooh kept his eyes alert on the streets looking for anything that seemed out of place. Every now and then he would glance back down to his phone to see what Lil Duke was talking about along with the comments that were coming at the bottom of his Instagram page.

Lil Duke stood in front of the camera with two Grape Street killas behind him. Both men had purple bandanas wrapped around their faces with assault rifles in their hands. Lil Duke stuck a MP 90 into the camera. "Y'all see dis shit right hurr, mane? Dis that mafucka that's gon' put them Choppa Gang niggas on they back when we slide. Dem bitch ass niggaz wanna drop innocent women now and shit, lil' kids and all of dat, awright den, two can play at dat game." Lil Duke smiled as he threw up a bunch of disrespectful gang signs to show his dismissal toward Choppa Gang, Cane Creek and Bread Gang. "This EBK, nigga. We *Every Body Killa* and fuck what you heard. "Say Pooh, Miss Gladyss just got put on the menu, look at this shit right hurr." Lil Duke held a gray wig in his hand. "Somebody thought they was gon' be able to wear this bitch to church. N'all, my nigga, it ain't happening."

Pooh perked up in the passenger's seat watching the live video. "Say mane, I know that nigga ain't got my mama, Slime."

Three-O frowned, "what? Fuck is you talking about?"

"Let me see yo' phone, hurry up." Pooh ordered, almost getting ready to panic.

Three-O dug it out of his Balmain jeans and handed it over to him. "Here, what the fuck is you sweating so bad for?"

Pooh called his mother right away. When she didn't pick up her cellphone, he left her message after message. He hung up and tried again. Lil Duke's Instagram video ended, and the next thing Pooh knew, Lil Duke was answering the phone via Facetime. Pooh's heart sank into the pit of his stomach.

"Well, well, well, I know damn well you bitch ass niggaz ain't thank that y'all was the only one who could get on gorilla mode. If you did, y'all got to be the dumbest niggaz in history, that's on gang." Lil Duke jacked.

Pooh dropped his phone and stuck his face into Three-O's, "bitch, if you touch my mama on everythang I love you finna have to move yo' people up out of Memphis, and the south period. I'ma murder your newborn lil girl nigga, now fuck wit it!"

Lil Duke started to laugh. He grabbed Miss Gladyss' by her hair and slung her to the floor in front of him before he took a shotgun and placed the barrel to her cheek. "All that woofing and shit the set don't get into dat. Bitch, I got some demands if you wanna see yo' mama alive again. If not, I'll just blow dis bitch head off right hurr and right now, fuck it. What you gon' do?"

"Pussy ass nigga, let Miss Gladyss go. That's a church woman. She don't mess wit' nobody. What the fuck is wrong wit' you?" Three-O snapped, slamming on the brakes in the middle of the street with two cars behind him that were now honking their horns impatiently.

Lil Duke kicked Miss Gladyss in the stomach, flipping her over on to her back. He placed his Balenciaga on her throat and pressed the barrel of the shotgun to her forehead again. "You thank I give two fucks about this bitch. I'm Muslim. I'll Allahu Akbar this punk bitch right now. What the fuck you gon' do, Pooh? Time is ticking?" Lil Duke cocked his pump.

"Whoa, whoa, whoa nigga, damn." Sweat slid down the sides of Pooh's face. He imagined his mother's brains being blown out on account of him and almost threw up. "What you want?"

Lil Duke smiled, "yeah, every nigga mother is his weakness. I should have snatched this bitch up a long time ago as vulnerable as you keep this ho. Fuck type of street nigga, is you?"

"What the fuck do you want!" Pooh hollered.

Lil Duke faced the camera, "since I know you Cane Creek niggas ain't really shit but a bunch of fucked up, broke ass jack boys, I ain't even about to ask you for no money cause that's an impossible task." He laughed for a moment and pressed the big barrel more firmly into Miss Gladyss's cheek. She whined for Pooh to help her. Lil Duke mugged Pooh. "Nigga, I want you to take yo' gun right now and drop both of those lil' Choppa Gang niggas I'm looking at in the back of your car. Turn around and stank they ass. If you don't I'ma kill this old bitch."

"What nigga?" Pooh slipped his F&N out of his waistband. "What the fuck I look like slumping my lil' niggaz for yo' bitch ass? This is loyalty over everythang over hurr."

"Oh yeah nigga, awright den." Lil Duke frowned and placed his finger over the trigger ready to blow.

"Nooooo!" Pooh turned around and started firing his gun. He pumped bullet after bullet into the seventeen and nineteen-year-old recruits that he and Three-O had just added to Choppa Gang. They fell against the seat before they sank to the floor in a bloody mess. Pooh glided the phone over their corpses. "They dead, mane. Ain't neither one of these niggaz moving. I did what you said, now let my mama go."

Lil Duke shook his head, "now kill Three-O. Hurry the fuck up. Pop that nigga or I'm slumping yo' bitch ass mama with no regard."

Three-O upped his Glock ready for Pooh to make an ill-advised move. "Say shawty, this nigga playing a game wit' you right now. Don't even try dat shit."

Pooh was stuck. "I ain't killing my home boy. You got me fucked up."

"N'all bitch, you got me fucked up. Here go some *LIVE* and in living color shit for you. Gang, hold that camera right here over her face. Yeah, just like that. That's perfect." Lil Duke told his young steppers. "Choppa Gang killa, Shiesty Gang killa, Bread Gang killa, Grape Street, bitch!"

Boom! Boom!

Two shotgun slugs blew Ms. Gladyss's face halfway off. Blood flew all over the camera lense. She laid on her back kicking like crazy. Lil Duke placed the barrel into her mouth and pulled the trigger again, killing her. He grabbed the phone, "how many pints we sippin' on now, nigga? You fuck niggaz wanted war you about to get it. Three-O you next, nigga. Y'all kilt my brother, you next Three-O!" The live froze and then disconnected.

Pooh opened the door of the car and ran over to the grass purging his guts. He fell to his knees in tears. "Not my moms, man. That's all I had left. Fuck! Fuck! *Fuck!*"

Three-O pulled the car to the side of the road and got out. He rushed to Pooh's side. "Damn, my nigga. You already know we ain't about to let that shit ride. We can handle it however you want to. What the fuck you wanna do?"

Pooh waved him off. "I'm sick right now, gang. I can't even thank straight. I'ma need a minute. Please, mane." He waved him away.

Cars pulled around Three-O's SRT. The back door had blood dripping from it. Three-O shook his head. *Damn, that lil' bitch ass nigga came hard*, he thought. He worried about Lil Duke clapping at him before he could get the chance to wipe him off the earth. As he was lost in deep thought, he saw two Cherry Caprice Classics turn on to the block at the far end. On the windowsills, were four shooters with Purple bandanas covering their faces with assault rifles in their hands. Three-O grabbed Pooh. "It's a hit my nigga, get yo' ass up." He took off running.

Pooh looked down the block and saw the opp's cars rolling his way. He got up and ran back to the SRT. He grabbed the Draco out of it and ran toward them. "Bitch ass niggaz!"

Bocka! Bocka! Bocka! Bocka!

His bullets shattered the first car's windshield. The car swerved and hit a parked car. Smoke sailed from its hood. Pooh ran directly at them still bussing his gun on a kamikaze mission. 'Y'all wanna fuck wit me?"

One of the shooters fell into the street after the Chevy crashed. He struggled to regain his composure but not before he caught three to the neck. He twisted and fell flat. Pooh caught another shooter trying to kneel and clap at him. That one caught one directly to the forehead. Pooh jumped up to the first car's hood and aired into the interior of it chopping down the rest of the killas inside of it.

The second car backed all of the way up at full speed and made a backwards u-turn, then it burned tires in its retreat. Pooh jumped off of the first car and chased the second one down the street bussing back to back. "Yeah niggaz! *Yeah!* Choppa Gang, hoe. Ain't shit sweet!" He stopped halfway down the block out of breath. Police sirens sounded in the distance.

Three-O pulled the SRT up. "Get yo' ass in nigga. Here comes Twelve."

Pooh stood there for a moment looking over all of the carnage that he'd caused. "Mane, we gotta erase those niggaz, Three-O. You hurr what the fuck I'm saying right now?"

Three-O nodded, "yeah, but for right now we need to get the fuck out of here. Come on, Slime."

"Awright, nigga." Pooh jumped in the car. As soon as Three-O stepped on the gas, tears spurt out of Pooh's eyes. "Kilt my mafuckin' mama, mane. I'm all fucked up."

Chapter 14

It was a dark, rainy night with occasional lighting that flashed across the sky. MayBaby had never felt more nervous in all of her life. She pulled her Chanel hoodie over her head and checked the time on her Audemars-Piguet.

Rondo was running late. He was supposed to have met up with her over twenty minutes ago and he had yet to answer his phone. "Damn, I should have never reached out to this dumb ass nigga for this meeting. What the fuck was I thanking?"

Rondo jogged through the crowd of pedestrians and headed to the Pier as the rain began to pick up and pitter patter the concrete. He spotted MayBaby standing just off of the dock next to the Ferry that was supposed to take them on a tour along the river. He caught up to her and placed his hand on her shoulder making her jump and turn around with her fists balled, ready for war.

"Chill out shawty, it's just me. I'm running a lil' late."

"Ya think?" She snapped, swiping his hand off of her. She pulled her hood tauter over her head and looked all around to make sure that nobody had followed Rondo.

Rondo looked over her shoulder toward the Ferry that was boarding. "Come on lil' one, let's make this voyage so we can talk bidness." He tried to take a hold of her hand, but she snatched it away from him. "What the fuck is yo' problem, bitch? You called me?"

MayBaby continued to scan the area. "I gotta make sure he ain't on our ass, and watch yo' mafuckin' mouth, Rondo. You know I ain't never came at you bogus. Show me some respect." She took a hold of his hand and looked into his eyes demandingly.

Rondo nodded and led them onto the boat. He paid the fare and they walked all around until they found a nice table at the bottom of the vessel. There was a low-lit lounge down there with a live jazz band that serenaded the patrons. Once there, MayBaby pulled her hood back and ran her fingers through her hair. She was a bit thrown off for cavorting with Jimmy Band's opp. She took a deep breath. She was already in too deep. It was best to finish the mission.

"So, what's good, shawty? I'm here. What's on yo' mind?"

"Before I even begin, I need to know somethin'?"

"Awright, what's that?" Rondo signaled for the waitress. When she came, he told her to bring them a bottle of Ducè.

MayBaby waited until the small white lady left and came back with their order before she continued. "I need to know what made you cross Jimmy after all he's done for you?"

"Shawty, you mean to tell me that you called me all the way over here just so you can do his bidding for him?" Rondo was immediately irritated.

"N'all, that nigga can do his own bidding. The reason I called you over hurr is cause I wanna work somethin' out wit' you, but before I do I need to know what kind of snake I'm actually dealing with?"

"That nigga Jimmy wasn't doing nothing for me that I couldn't do for myself. Every penny I made, every opp I dropped was in honor of him and he paid me crumbs. Once I really started to see what type of time he was on, I ain't have no interest in running behind that nigga no more. I don't see how you still do as much as he puts his foot up yo' ass."

MayBaby placed a tuft of hair behind her ear and looked away. "How Jimmy Bands handles me is my business. It doesn't have anything to do with you."

"Yeah, well, that's good to know cause there were a bunch of times I wanted to put his ass down on account of you. I never did like to see a nigga putting his hands on a female, especially when she didn't deserve it. Most times that nigga would whoop you and you didn't even do shit wrong." He shook his head.

"Well, I didn't call you here to ask your opinion of how Jimmy and I's relationship made you feel. I called you here because I'm ready to leave Jimmy, but I don't want to do it blindly."

"What do you mean?"

"Well, I've been with him for what seems like an eternity. I've become accustomed to a certain lifestyle. One that I don't want to honestly give back, but it's come to the point where I thank he's going to kill me one of these days."

"Damn, that's fucked up."

"I don't need your sympathies, thank you very much." She rolled her eyes.

"So, what do you want from me? Keep in mind that I don't trust yo' ass as far as I can throw you either. I'm just keeping that shit real."

"Nigga, I don't trust you either. I don't know what would make you thank I do."

"Why do you want from me?" He became angry at the back and forth.

"Shhh. Damn boy, you got every Tom, Dick and Harry looking at us."

Rondo stood up, "bitch, I should have one of the hoez from the hood stomp a mud hole in yo' ass and throw you in my crocodile pit. Don't ever contact me again. If you ever call me playing games like you are right now, I'ma put you down just like I'ma do his ass when I slide on him." He started to walk away from the table.

"I wanna make sho' you become the king of Orange Mound and the Duffel Bag Cartel. I know that I can because I have what everybody wants, but before I do any of that I need some reassurances from you."

Rondo stopped in his tracks and turned around. "What can you possibly have that's gon' ensure that?"

"What type of reassurances can you give me first? I need to know what it looks like with you in charge of the Duffle Bag Cartel. What does that look like for me?"

Rondo took his seat and mugged her. "What do you want?"

"Before you fully take the throne, I need three million dollars and then once you step into royalty, I want twenty thousand a month for as long as you're in power. Even though I know you have that cutthroat shit in you, you've always been a man of your word, at least that's what the streets say, so I need your word."

"My word? MayBaby, you still ain't told me how you're going to make sure I take over everythang. I ain't promisin' you shit until you tell me dat."

MayBaby reached into her bag and slid a quarter ounce of the Rebirth over to him. "That there is gold."

Rondo held it up and looked it over without exposing the package to the rest of the people that were chilling in the dimly lit lounge area. "What the fuck is this?"

"That, my friend, is the Rebirth."

"You shitting me." He looked it over closer.

"Not only do I know where a thousand kilos of the Rebirth are right now, but I also know when and where they will be arriving right here in Memphis. I already have it set up to where you and a few of your men could easily take over everything before it even touches either Phoenix or Jimmy Bands' hands. The worst thang a man can do is hurt the woman he pillow talks with. I am the thread that is holding both Jimmy Bands and Phoenix's throne together. Right now, as we speak,

Phoenix is laid up with my little sister, Cassie, and he doesn't even know it. The Stevens' dote off of forbidden pussy. That is their weakness right there. It's been like that with them since the beginning of time."

Rondo stroked his chin hairs. "And you're absolutely sure that this shit is one hunnit? What assurances do you have?"

"All I have is my word as a woman. I know you are deadly, and I know that there is a war waging between you and the Duffle Bag Cartel. That man you saw in the mansion was none other than Taurus Stevens. That's as high up as it gets, and you've crossed him and wound up on his radar of adversaries."

"Fuck that nigga. I don't give a fuck about him or nobody else. Plus, there are a slew of kingpins that just upped the fee to fifteen million for his head and the head of his daughter. I wish I could get my hands on them; I'd kill three birds with one Glock." He sucked his gold teeth. "Bitch, I ain't paying you no three million dollars until the Rebirth is in my hands, or at least I get the drop of the location and confirm that it's there. Before we do anythang, I need to know that all of this shit is one hunnit"

"That's understandable. I wouldn't have it any other way." She snatched the bottle of Ducè from the table and poured a half glass of it.

"You talking about you wanna know what level of snake you're dealing with when I'm wondering the same damn thang. How are you going to go and sleep up under this nigga until all of this shit happen, knowing it's about to happen?"

She was quiet for a moment. "Many times, as Jimmy Bands done kicked my ass, he's knocked the love, loyalty, and devotion right out of me. I can't even thank straight no mo. I'm solidifying my future is all dat I'm doing. You can't blame a girl for doing such thangs and even if you did, you can kiss my ass."

Rondo mugged her for a long time, and then he busted up laughing. He slapped the table with his hand and kept cackling. "I like yo style MayBaby, I never thought that I'd say nothing like dat bout you, but I like it and I had to admit it."

***

Cassie filled her mug with hot chocolate and added marshmallows to the top. She placed it on a platter alongside Phoenix's. She bust open a well whipped fentanyl pill and dropped it into his drink, stirring it with a small spoon while she rubber necked to see inside of the living room.

She noted that he was still sitting on the couch watching the Olympics. She slipped beside him and set the drinks on the table. "Here you go, cuz. I made us a little hot cocoa. I've always wanted to sip hot cocoa and chill in a Lodge, but of course we never had money to do anything like that."

Phoenix scrolled down his messenger. "I don't drank no chocolate, shawty. All that sweet shit ain't my thang. But you go right ahead though."

Cassie's mood dropped. *How the fuck am I going to hold up my end of every thang if I can't get him to snooze,* she wondered sipping out of her own mug. "Okay, cuz. Well, what do you wanna do? I thought you had somethin' real special planned for me."

Phoenix responded to a few messages from Jimmy Bands. He had yet to find and kill Rondo and that was pissing him off. When it came to the game threats, had to be put down right away. The longer you waited the stronger the opp seemed to become. That was a detriment to the Duffle Bag Cartel especially with such a large shipment of the Rebirth set to hit Memphis. "Shawty, I just thought we would kick back and chill, you know get to know each other a little bit, unless you got something else on your mind." He turned his phone off and placed it inside of his pocket.

Cassie hopped up. "Well, if we gon' kick it, why can't we go somewhere outside? My mama keeps me cooped up in the house so much that it's irritating. I wanna do somethin' different." She had a few places she could lure Phoenix where the savages from Cane Creek could get a hold of him now that she saw that it was going to be nearly impossible for her to get him incapacitated herself.

"Lil' One, where you wanna go? You wanna fuck around at the Tennessee State Fair? Huh? You want a mafucka to go and win you some of those stuffed animals and shit?"

Cassie rubbed her chin. The Tennessee State Fair was only a few miles away from her projects. She was sure she could call up a few hittas from the deck and they would handle Phoenix and she would still be able to get her hundred thousand dollars cut. Both herself and her mother needed it.

Cassie was tired of staying in the projects. She wanted to travel. She yearned to leave Memphis behind. She was tired of the city and all the murders. "I mean, if you thank you could show me a good time by taking me out dem ways den yeah, let's do it. I'll go get dressed." She hopped up and grabbed her cellphone off the table taking it into the bedroom with her where she planned to have Phoenix trunked.

Phoenix grabbed thirty thousand dollars in cash out of his safe and the keys to his newly released Bugatti, hard drop. He showered and tossed on a Balenciaga fit with the snake skinned Balenciaga shoes that offset the four pounds of gold and ice around his neck. On his right wrist was an AP skeleton with all-white VVS diamonds and on his left wrist was an Audemars-Piguet with all-black blood diamonds. Cartier frames covered his eyes. When he stepped out of the bath-room, Cassie couldn't help her jaws from dropping. "Say shawty, you ready to hit the strip?"

Cassie looked him up and down, and then thought about the get up she had on. Suddenly, she felt like a bum. "I can't go out there looking like this."

"Like what, Lil' One?"

"Like ass while you look like class. We're better off staying in." She sat down on the couch and crossed her arms in front of her chest.

Phoenix laughed and took his frames off. "Shawty, you're my lil' cousin, right?"

"You damn right I am. Excuse me Lord, for my language."

"Well, I'ma get you together, don't even trip. But I just took yo' ass shopping. Why didn't you ask for some shit like what I'm wearing?"

"Because it's expensive. I didn't think that it was even an option. You would blow a bag like that on me?"

Phoenix nodded. "This shit chump change. This is what the fuck I do. You wanna go hard then we gon' get you together. You my lil' cousin. We can't have no Stevens running around looking all popped and shit. I got you, come gimme a hug."

Cassie hopped up and closed her arms around him. She hugged him warmly with his jewelry making all kinds of noise every time it moved in the slightest. "I appreciate you already, Phoenix. I don't know why you care about me so much, but I definitely appreciate you."

Chapter 15

MayBaby eased into the Townhouse off Brookshire. She found Jimmy Bands at the table in the middle of the living room snoring loudly. In front of him was a broken kilo of heroin, a razor blade, a mirror, and his F&N. The radio bellowed a Yo Gotti tune and she could smell that it had been a few days since Jimmy Bands had been in the shower. She was about to slip past him and up to their bedroom when his eyes popped open. "Where the fuck you been at?"

MayBaby paused in her tracks. "I had to run a few errands with my sister, and then it started to rain really hard so I waited for the storm to die down. You already know how bad my eyes are. I can't drive when it gets so bad."

Jimmy Bands ran his hand over his face. "Sounds like some bullshit to me is what it sounds like, but I don't even give a fuck. Don't take yo' ass upstairs either."

MayBaby frowned. "Why can't I go to our room?"

"Cause I got a young bitch up there and I ain't done with her yet. Her mama came short on the dope, and I just had to have her, baby. You already know how this shit goes." He got a line ready to be tooted. "She got some good pussy, too. Dese days you gotta catch 'em young because by the time they get to be fifteen, their pussy already ain't no good. Every dope boy on this side of the states done fucked 'em by dat time."

MayBaby scrunched her face. "So, I'm supposed to *not* go up to my room because you have a child up there."

"It ain't yo' room, it's mine. You ain't paid a bill since I met yo' ass, and you ain't got nothing but the income I give yo' ass. That's what I said, so find you somewhere else to sleep."

MayBaby nodded. "Okay, I'll do that. I sho' don't feel like arguing wit' you. Can I at least go and get some sheets and blankets for the guest room?"

Jimmy Bands had nodded back out. He snored so loud that it quickly became annoying. "I don't give a fuck what you do. Just leave me alone for the moment. Can't you see I'm enjoying my shit, bitch?"

MayBaby ignored him as he leaned his head forward to snort two more lines. She made her way up the stairs and down the hallway where the linen closet was located. She grabbed the door handle and stopped. She waited to see if Jimmy Bands was going to follow her. When he didn't, she crept back down the hallway and peeked over the banister at him. He nodded back out.

She crept to their bedroom door and slowly opened it. When she looked inside and saw the small naked child laying on her stomach playing a video game on an iPad, she became faint. MayBaby eased further into the room. The little girl thought she was Jimmy Bands coming back so she slid the iPad under the pillow and laid on her back opening her thighs for him with her eyes closed. MayBaby shook her head and eased out of the room. She had seen enough. She closed the door and headed back down the stairs. Jimmy Bands was up now dancing to an old Avant song. When he saw her, he grabbed her and turned her around in a circle before he dipped her.

MayBaby laughed as if she was enjoying the moment. Then she spun out of his embrace and sat on the couch. "Jimmy, we need to talk business. I know it's usually my job to make sure I have a team of sorters and baggers ready for when the shipment of the Rebirth comes in, and I want to make sure I have them ready ahead of time this time. When does everybody need to be assembled and ready?"

Jimmy Bands staggered for a moment drinking from his double cup of pink Sprite. "In two weeks." He laughed. "I got so much dope coming through this bitch the Wednesday after next that I'ma be able to take over Memphis, Tennessee, Texas, Arkansas, Mississippi, and even Georgia. I got plans, shawty. I'm so geeked up that I can't thank straight. That's why I've been doing this dope like ninety going north."

"So, by next Wednesday then, are you sho?"

"Am I sho? Yeah bitch, I'm sho'. The dope geniuses are already in the lab and Phoenix gave me the order. Mafuckas been paid and we about to get ours. Ooowe! I can't wait, baby." He flopped on the couch and leaned his head back on the cushion. "Bitch, make sho' you got at least eighty hoez like last time. We takin' over the old bread factory for a full week to make this happen. I already hit the police, an alderman and two senators over that way. We are good to go. You make sho' yo' ass is, too."

MayBaby smiled, "oh, I will be. That's one thing you don't have to worry about. I'll be on point." She got up and walked away rubbing her hands together.

***

The music coming from Phoenix's Bugatti caused the ground to shake as he rolled through the city of Memphis. Nearly every block he rolled down, women stopped and started to twerk just to catch his attention. They would turn their backs to him and pull their shorts deep into their asses and proceed to shake everything they had while he laughed.

Cassie found it annoying. Before they got to the State Fair, Cassie was able to purchase a pink and black Prada dress that complimented her frame, over black, red bottom Louis Vuittons. He placed a pink lemonade diamond tennis bracelet over her left wrist and a matching Cartier watch with crushed pink diamonds on her right. Her Cartier frames were wood, and she felt like a million bucks as they strolled through the fairgrounds stopping at every booth where she saw a cute stuffed animal. She spotted a big white teddy bear that held a heart in the middle of it and she felt that she had to have it.

Phoenix stepped up to the game and sized it up quickly. The sunlight reflected off of the diamonds around his neck and wrist. "Say mane, how many cents I gotta make before y'all give my cousin one of dem damn bears?"

The white man looked him up and down and knew that he had a victim on his hands. He spit chewing tobacco into a can and wiped his lips. "Need to make four of dem baskets so she can walk out of here wit' a big bear. You make one, she gets a little one. More ya make, bigger da prize. What you wanna do, Mister?"

Phoenix pulled out a knot of blue face hundreds. "I'd like to just buy her one, what's the price tag?"

The red-faced white man waved him off. "Dat ain't dat way it works. Ya gotta win to take it home. Step right up."

Phoenix scoffed. "Shawty, you sho' dats the one you want?"

"It sho' is and I don't want you to buy it. I want you to win it. Ain't nothing cool 'bout cheating."

Phoenix smiled. "Yeah, okay." He handed the man a fifty. "Since the balls are two dollars apiece give me twenty-five of dem bitchez and step back while I swish a few."

The man barely moved. "Shoot. You make four and you win the big one."

Phoenix squared up and shot the first one. It bounced off of the rim. He shot the second one, it hit the backboard and came off. The third rimmed in and then back out. "Say mane, I don't miss. You sho' that rim ain't too small for this ball?"

The white man grabbed the ball and dropped it through the hoop. "Oh, it fits. Just all about the shooter it seems like."

Phoenix mugged him. "Ain't a better shooter in all of Memphis. You better ask the slums about me."

"No need, you got twenty-two more balls. Shoot." The white man ordered.

Phoenix squared back up and shot ball after ball. One by one they rimmed in and out or hit the front of the rim. Before he knew it, he had shot all twenty-five balls and hadn't made a shot. "Gimme me twenty-five more. I see what I've been doing wrong."

The man gave him the balls and hit a switch on his key chain that widened the rim. He allowed Phoenix to make two shots and then he hit the button on the keychain again and tightened the rim back. Phoenix missed twenty-three in a row. He cursed out loud. The man grabbed the smallest keychain bear that he could and held it out to Phoenix.

"Man, I don't want that shit. I'm going for the big one. That's the one you want right, lil' cuz?" Phoenix asked.

"That's okay, Phoenix, let's just go." Cassie started to feel sorry for him.

"N'all, I got this. You see, I made two of them before. I got it." He bought another twenty-five balls. This time the white man waited until he got to his last three balls and activated the button that widened the rim all the way. Phoenix hit three in a row. He pulled out another fifty and shot until they were gone, missing all of them. He cursed loudly and shot daters at the white man who didn't so much as flinch. "Next! Sorry, pal."

"I ain't yo' pal, bitch, you don't know me." Phoenix hissed.

"Next!" The white man hollered.

"I'll go." A little white boy stepped up to shoot. The white man widened the rim as far as it could go. The boy hit four in a row, then four more before he missed his last two. The white man gave him two of the biggest bears that were hanging. The little white boy walked away with his arms full, happier than ever.

Phoenix stood there for a long time. He watched a black teen step up and start to shoot. He missed every shot before he stepped away. Then a Mexican missed every shot just the same. When a white female stepped up, Phoenix caught the movement of the game runner's thumb on the keychain. The white woman made all of her shots and was handed a big bear. Phoenix jolted and jumped over the counter of the game. He grabbed the keychain from the white man with one hand and snatched him up with the other. He pressed on the button and saw the rim tighten and loosen. "You sorry son of a bitch."

The white man began to panic. "Look, it is what it is, man. All the games are rigged, not just mine. How 'bout that bear, huh?"

Cassie was already filling her arms with bears of her choice. "Shame on you, Mister. Shame on you."

Phoenix hopped back one the counter. "Mane, let some minorities win at this shit, too. That's what exposed yo' stupid ass." He put his arm around Cassie's, kissed her cheek and they walked right out of the fair and hopped back in the Bugatti.

"Phoenix, can we roll through my hood for a spell? I wanna see my mama. I miss her and I was kinda hoping we could drop her off a meal or somethin'."

Phoenix instantly thought about the number of enemies he had over in the southeastern section of Memphis and decided against it. He'd been smoking the opp over in that region ever since he'd come to the city of Memphis from Arizona. "N'all shawty, I can't play wit' the opp like that. I'll Cash App yo' mama a few dollars or somethin' or send Uber Eats over that way. You and I are about to head back to my duck off. I got some bidness I need to take care of, and I need to be in a comfortable state of mind when I do it so let's roll out."

Cassie thought about the hundred thousand dollars that MayBaby had promised her if she could help to facilitate the setup of Phoenix. All Cassie needed to do was get Phoenix to the southeastern portion of Memphis or over to Orange Mound. Either region, the killers out that way would step in and come for his head according to MayBaby. "Well, can we at least roll through the Mound? I always wanted to see what that side of town looked like. Besides, ain't that where you're from?"

"Shawty, I'm originally from Arizona but my stomping grounds ever since I came to Tennessee have been Orange Mound. You really wanna roll through the hood?"

Cassie grew giddy. "Yeah, I thank that would be so cool to see how it looks. I ain't been too far outside of Cane Creek. I barely know what any of the cities look like no more."

Phoenix nodded. He had a few loyal killas on standby in Orange Mound. All he had to do was text them and have them meet him right at the border, then they could escort him into the projects and back out of them. That was their sole job and the reason they were on the Duffle Bag's payroll. "I got one better for you. My nigga, Dolph, roll into town tonight. He gon' be at the FedX Forum. I got backstage passes and front row seats for the homey. We gon' get flier than the rest of 'em and show up and support the homey. After the concert, we'll roll out to the Mound. I gotta put at least a quarter million dollars in jewels all over you first. After that, we'll show up and show out. How you like the sound of that?"

Cassie was in love with Dolph. She was crazy about his dark skin, his country grammar, and the fact that he was his own boss. Out of all the rappers that came from Memphis, Dolph was her favorite. She couldn't pass up the opportunity to see him. "Okay cousin, that sounds amazing. Let's do it."

"Awright den, that's what we on." Phoenix started the ignition and handed her his phone. "Order yo' mama some food and give me my shit back."

"Okay." Cassie did just that, then texted MayBaby and told her what their plans were for the night.

Chapter 16

Jahliyah straddled Taurus's waist while he laid on his stomach. She applied pressure to his back and rubbed all over it giving him the deepest massage. He groaned and closed his eyes. The feel of her hot box on him felt glorious. She leaned all the way down until her cheek was planted to his. "You like how that feels, Daddy?"

"Hell yeah, I do." Taurus flipped over and laid on his back. Jahliyah yelped when he suddenly pulled her down to him, catching her off guard. He brought her lips to his own. They kissed passionately. By the time they broke it, Jahliyah was panting hard, and Taurus was fully erect between her thighs with his piece knocking at her naked sex.

Natalia stepped into the living room and cleared her throat. "Well, well, well, what the *fuck* do we have here?" She snapped, squatting down beside their heads.

Jahliyah jumped up and grabbed her gown off the couch. She slipped it over her head and mugged Natalia. "What are you doing here?"

"I had a change of heart. I thought about what we talked about but then I remembered that I don't owe you a mutha-fuckin' thing, so why would I ever help you to do anything when you've been nothing but a thorn in my side ever since we've become a part of one another?"

Jahliyah rolled her eyes. "Here we go with the melodramatics. Ain't nobody got time for dis."

"You're right, cause your time is up. I want you out of here right the fuck now. Whatever you did wit' our father was yo' last time doing it. I should have known yo' triflin' ass had a hidden agenda. I didn't trust you from day one."

Taurus stood up and straightened himself up. "Natalia, shut that shit up. She ain't going nowhere. That's not for you to say."

Natalia was taken aback. Jahliyah smiled. Natalia side-stepped Jahliyah and stepped one a few inches from Taurus. "Oh, so now you're choosing her over me all because y'all have had a few days together screwing and doing all of this other shit? This is how you're going to do me, Daddy?"

Taurus became angry. He took a hold of her arm and pulled her upstairs all the while with her telling him that he was hurting her. He ignored her. When they got in the room, he slammed the door and faced her. Natalia already had tears in her eyes. She covered her face with her hands. Taurus felt sick.

"How could you, Daddy? How could you love her in the same way you love me? I thought what we had was special. But I see it wasn't. You broke my heart." She fell to her knees and cried her eyes out.

Taurus looked up to the ceiling as if he could see heaven and cursed under his breath. "Damn," he dropped to his knees in front of her. "Natalia, baby, don't do this. I'm begging you not to."

"I thought I was special. I thought you loved me in our own way, but then you did everything with her that you did with me. You even did more. You told her that her birth meant the most. You said she was your life. That means I'm nothing. It means all of this was for nothing, Daddy. The finding you, the paying of millions for your fresh start, the killing off all my rivals, including my mother and naming my son after you. None of it means anything anymore because you don't love me the most. You never have and you never will. I hate you. I swear to God, I hate you with all of my soul." She burst into a temper tantrum of sobbing, beating her fist on the ground over and over while she cried.

Taurus pulled her to him. "Natalia, why does it have to be this way? Why can't I love both of *my* daughters the same? Why can't we be a family the way we are supposed to?"

"Because it doesn't work like that. You have to choose. You can only love one of us in the right way, it can't be both. It's not gonna work like that. But now, after you slept with her and made all kinds of love to her body, I don't know if I even want anything to do with you anymore, matter of fact, get away from me." She pushed him and stood up pacing back and forth.

Taurus slowly came to his feet. He sighed. Jahliyah knocked on the door and stuck her head inside of the room. Taurus invited her in and closed the door. Jahliyah stepped next to him and expected him to place his arm around her shoulders which he did.

Natalia saw this and stopped her pacing. "I swear to God, the more I look at you two together the more I hate the both of you. I wish I would have never come looking for you, Daddy. I wish my mother never told me you were even my father. You have hurt me ten times more than any man I have ever crossed paths with!" She got into Jahliyah's face. "And you, with your goody two shoes persona, your perfect body, and dimples. I'm gonna get you back for how you finessed me into leaving you alone with him so you could *steal* him. I watched you in action. I saw how you seduced him and played the curious little girl role to the tee. I bet you had all of this mapped out, didn't you? This was your very plan from the start *wasn't* it!"

Jahliyah backed up and held her arms straight out. "Sis, it ain't even nothing like that. The only person that's looking at this situation as a conspiracy is you. Truth be told, neither one of us should be sleeping with him, and we definitely shouldn't be falling in love or trying to get him to love one daughter more than the other. We're all family and all that either of us have. I don't wish to beef with you anymore. You are my sister and I want to call a truce. Couldn't all of us go back to normal?"

Natalia mugged her. "There has never been a normal for me, Jahliyah. I don't know what that is. My whole life I've been abused by one person after the next. Nobody has ever truly loved me unconditionally, so what the fuck does normal even mean?"

Taurus tried to take a hold of her hand. "Baby, come here."

She jerked away from him. "I'm not your baby, she is. My name is Natalia." She crossed her arms again and turned her back to him.

Jahliyah placed her hand on her shoulder. "My sister today is the first day for the rest of our lives. Listen to me, I love you. You don't owe me anything. All I ask is for you to give us a chance at being real sisters. Let's be there for each other instead of plotting against one another. I wanna have your back."

"Jahliyah, although that may sound good, nah. My whole life all I've ever had looking out for me was me. I have never trusted anybody because sooner or later they let you down." She turned around and looked into Taurus's eyes. "About the only thing I can accept from either of you right now is an apology."

"A what?" Jahliyah was defiant. She placed her hand on her hip and looked at Natalia as if she were out of her mind.

"An apology. Jahliyah, you said you and Taurus would never sleep together. You said that the thought wasn't even on your mind, yet before I could get off the street good enough you were already stripping and climbing into the shower with him.

"How did you know that?" Jahliyah was shocked and confused.

"And you, *Daddy*. You said you loved me. You said I was your lil' baby. You said what we had was special and you would never leave nor forsake me. You said you would never hurt me. Yet, here I am hurt, left, and forsaken. How could you do me like this? Especially knowing all I have been through."

Taurus yanked her to him aggressively. He snatched her up and against the wall. "Natalia, stop talking that dumb shit. I love yo' lil' ass and you are my heart. Just because I love Jahliyah as well doesn't mean I don't love you every bit as much as I told you I do. Stop this nonsense and quit creating this unnecessary ass division because it's getting old. Do you hear me?"

Natalia looked into his eyes. "Is this the way you treat a woman you love? Is this how princesses are treated behind closed doors because if it is, I no longer want to be your princess." Tears slid down her face. "Take your hands off me, Taurus. Please, or I can't be held responsible for what I do to you."

Taurus tightened his grip. "'Stop this shit. You hear me, stop it. Enough is enough." He shook her just a bit.

Jahliyah pried Taurus's hands loose. "Let her go, Daddy. Anger isn't going to solve anything."

"I'm not mad. I just need her to snap out of it. This is not the way it's supposed to be." Taurus said, eyeing Natalia.

"How did you think this was going to go, huh? You know once you put your dick in me?" Natalia asked.

"Natalia, plcase baby, enough is enough." Taurus was growing more impatient by the second.

"Did you think that I would just be that daughter you could fuck when you wanted to with no strings attached? What, you think feelings wouldn't develop? How am I supposed to be right now when you have *fucked* unhealthy emotions into me the way you have? Answer me, Taurus!" Natalia demanded, taking her finger and poking him in the chest with it.

Jahliyah took a step back and covered her mouth. She honestly wanted to know what Taurus's response was going to be. Her sister made a good stance as much as she hated to admit that. Taurus hung his head. His chest heaved up and down. He shrugged and remained silent.

"You see, that's what I thought. You don't know what to say because when all these same things happened between you and your mother, she probably didn't have a response for you either, and this is probably why we're all here right now. I've read all of the *Raised As A Goon* books, Daddy. This isn't nothing but the cycle repeating itself. You didn't break it, instead you passed it down to both myself and my sister right here. So, let me ask you something, Jahliyah, now that you've fucked our father how do you feel? Better or worse than you did previously?"

Chapter 17

"I really don't want to be in the middle of this conversation, Natalia. Whatever y'all have going on is between y'all. I don't want any parts of it." Jahliyah threw her hands up and turned around to sit down.

"N'all, fuck that, Jahliyah. You don't get to sit back and wait until me and Dad's relationship completely crumbles while you remain silent. You need to be a part of it because that's the only way he's going to know the effect that lying down with us is doing to us emotionally. So please, tell him how you feel."

"I don't feel like nothing. I mean I enjoyed our time together, and if you hadn't come through and broken up the party, I feel like we would have still been chilling, drama free. I didn't do anything with him that I didn't want to do. To be quite honest, it has been on my mind since before I got here from New York and now that it's happened, it is what it is. You forget, I'm originally from Memphis, whether you know it or not this is the norm. It's just that most people keep it behind closed doors and our family's business is in the streets because we come from a long line of king pins and stick-up kids."

Natalia waved her off. "Yeah, all of that sounds good and it's the truth, but that's not what I'm getting at. What I'm asking you, Jahliyah, is do you feel like you have sacrificed yourself and your morals to get the love from our father that you have always craved?"

Jahliyah was silent for a moment. She shrugged. "I don't know. I don't want to feel like that, but I guess a slight part of me does even though I did enjoy everything I did with him. I guess I just feel like if he and I hadn't done the deed, you would have forever had him wrapped around your little finger, and I couldn't allow that because after losing my mother, he and JaMichael are all I have."

Natalia sneered at her. "I knew you had a hidden agenda. You bitch, I saw it all along."

Taurus stepped up to Jahliyah and pulled her to her feet. "Baby, I swear I ain't never want you thanking like that. I'm at a loss for words because I know damn well, I should have had more self-restraint than I did. I guess that DNA inside of me really is rotten."

Natalia frowned and pulled him to her. "Why are you only apologizing to Jahliyah? Don't you think I deserve one, too, huh? She's not the only one who's hurting right now. I was hurting first; let's not forget that fact."

Taurus sighed and nodded, "you're right, Natalia. I'm sorr–."

"There you go using my name again. Every time you refer to Jahliyah, it's baby or Boo Boo, but you use my name. Damn, that tells me everything I need to know. You've fucked this bitch for a day or so and now you love her the most, even though I done did all this shit for you. I just don't get it. What does she have over me? What Daddy!"

"Natalia, calm down. Nobody has anything over the other one. I love both of you the same. It's my own fault that we are here right now." Taurus took a hold of her shoulders so he could look into her eyes.

Natalia couldn't keep her anger from surging. She pushed him away and turned to Jahliyah. "Bitch, you think you're better than me because you're all caramel and shit, huh? You think you're better because your dimples are deeper than mine and you don't have a few of these on your stomach." Natalia lifted her shirt and ran her hand across her stomach that was decorated with a few stretch marks from her pregnancy with

Taurus Jr. Though they were there, they were faint, and her abs showed clear as day under them.

"Girl, I don't know what you talking about. I don't think I'm better than you. I have never said that, and I will never feel like that. You are my sister and even though you are evil as sin, I love you."

Natalia staggered backward. "You love me? You *love* me?" She wagged her finger at her. "N'all, Jahliyah, you're up to something. You see, I know your type. You use words to weaken and dismantle. If I buy into the bullshit that you're selling, you're going to find a way to capitalize off of my ignorance, but I refuse to give you that satisfaction, so this is how this is going to go. You are going to pack your shit and take yo' black ass back to New York. If I ever catch you anywhere near him again, I'm going to kill you in cold blood. You hear me?" She stepped into her face. "I'm going to slice your pretty face repeatedly before I perform an autopsy on you ripping out that fuckin' heart of yours. I have given you enough passes. Now, it's time to get on some straight gangsta shit."

Jahliyah smirked, "dats what we on?" She rolled up her hair and tucked it into a bun. "Okay den, since you talkin' like that." She swung and slapped Natalia so hard that she dazed her. Jahliyah rushed her and picked her up into the air, slamming her back to the floor knocking the wind out of her. She stood up, "what bitch? This ain't that. I'm tired of yo' mouth. I can't keep playing pussy. You got me fucked up!"

Taurus rushed over and picked Jahliyah up off her feet. He carried her to the end of the living room and set her down. "Baby, what the fuck?"

Jahliyah was in a zone. "Daddy, I love you, but I don't want to hear that right now. She runs her mouth way too much. All she does all day long is pop off. I ain't about to let nobody tell me what to do unless they are helping me pay my bills, which she ain't. And I'm damn sho' not married to em'. Ain't no punk in me."

Taurus couldn't help but see Princess coming out of Jahliyah. Princess was a lethal savage with no regard and zero tolerance for disrespect. He grabbed Jahliyah and pulled her to him, holding her. "Damn, this is all my fault."

Jahliyah wiggled up out of his embrace. "No, it ain't. Sooner or later, somebody needed to give her ass a reality check."

Natalia slowly climbed to her feet. She mugged Jahliyah, she laughed and touched the corners of her mouth that dripped blood. She looked over her fingers and nodded. "Bitch, you got me bleeding. Okay, this just upped the stakes. Now, it's on." She flipped the living room table and held up her guards.

Jahliyah threw her guards up and advanced toward her. "Bitch, you ain't said shit but a few words."

"This ain't about to happen, y'all can cut this out right now." Taurus got in the middle of them.

"Move, Daddy. It's too late. Get out of the way. We're both grown. You gotta let us get this out of our system." Natalia said, wrapping her waist length hair up and tucking it inside of her shirt.

"Yeah, Daddy. We'll be good after this." Jahliyah wanted her sister's ass, and there was no way Taurus was going to stop her from getting it.

***

Cassie pumped her fist in the air repeatedly as Dolph performed his last hit on the stage. After finishing up he was escorted off it by his numerous security guards. The crowd went crazy. Cassie was so happy. She'd had the time of her life. She turned to Phoenix and threw her arms around his neck as the crowd around her began to file out of the building. "That was awesome. Damn he did his thing. Ain't nobody messin' wit' Dolph. That was so amazing."

Phoenix smiled and placed his arm around her shoulders. "I'm glad you liked it shawty. That's what it's all about. He scanned the crowd checking for potential jackers, or enemies that always seemed to pop up out of the blue in Memphis. It was one of the reasons he didn't go to certain events, but Cassie felt worth it to him.

"Man, I can't wait for Lil' Baby and Durk to come to town. Their new album is hot. You thank we'll be able to hit up that concert, too?"

Phoenix nodded. "It's whatever, shawty. We just gon' have to see what it do when the time comes." They continued to make their way through the crowded arena. Phoenix was reminding himself next time to make sure he left before the last song because the bumping into other people, and the rubbing elbows was starting to get on his nerves.

Three people had already stepped on his thirty-five-hundred-dollar kicks and neither of them excused themselves. He saw more than a few females that he'd curbed and was praying that none of them stopped to cause a scene. He simply wanted to get out of there so he could get Cassie alone to see what she was all about. She'd stood in front of him the entire concert dancing and backing that rounded backside into his front. More than once, he'd taken a hold of her hips and allowed her to pop her ass. She felt glorious and he was ready to take it there with her.

As they got to the parking lot, Cassie wrapped her arm within his and stayed close. "Do you remember where we parked?"

Phoenix rubber necked, once again searching the crowd in front of them. "Yeah shawty, we up thurr in row G. I remember 'cause I parked there on purpose but let me make sho' though." He released her arm and dug into his pocket. He pulled out twenty thousand dollars in cash searching for the parking ticket. It wasn't in the first pocket, so he searched the second one pulling out twenty-five thousand in cash. The ticket fell on the ground. Cassie reached down to pick it up. She stood and handed it to Phoenix. As he was taking it from her, a Jack boy ran up and yanked all three chains from Phoenix's neck and took off running.

"Aw shit, this bitch ass nigga!" Phoenix took off after him.

"Phoenix!" Cassie screamed.

Phoenix was on a mission. He chased the robber as he zig zagged through the crowds thirty strides ahead of Phoenix. The robber wound up running out of the Forum's parking lot. He cut across the busy street and kept moving. Phoenix was wishing that he had his gun on him. His chest began to get tight. He saw the robber running full speed and gaining more of a distance. Phoenix's lungs felt like they were about to explode. He stopped running and hunched over breathing hard.

Cassie caught up to him and placed her hand on his back. "Are you okay, cuz?"

Phoenix struggled to catch his breath. "Hell n'all, that fuck nigga got away. Did you see his face?"

"N'all, it happened so fast. I didn't even thank to look." She tried to see where the jacker had gone but he was nowhere in sight. "What do we do now?"

Phoenix still struggled to breathe. "I don't know, but I gotta have a nigga head about mine. That was three million dollars' worth of jewelry. That's why I don't ever come to shit like this, cause fuck shit like this always happens."

Cassie dropped her head. "I'm sorry, cuz. I didn't know nothing like this was going to take place."

Phoenix walked off leaving her standing there for a moment until she started to jog behind him. By the time she caught up, he was already back at his Porsche. He hit the switch on his keychain to lift the Lamborghini doors. He sat down inside and started texting one of his shooters after the next. He placed a million-dollar bounty on his jewelry and for the nigga that caught him lacking. Upon the recovery of both bounty hunters, he would get a million dollars in cash from the Duffle Bag Cartel. Phoenix would personally make sure of it. "Get yo' ass in and let's get the fuck up out of here."

Cassie got into the car and pulled down the door attempting to slam it. "I don't know why you're all angry with me. I didn't do anything to you."

"I ain't mad at yo' lil' ass, so shut that shit up. I'm just irritated because my shit got taken. Three million in jewelry will put a mafucka on the map. That nigga probably gon' get every bit of five hundred thousand for my shit. If he goes out of town, he might even get a full million. I hate when a nigga tries to come up off me. That's all that there is to it right there. It ain't got nothing to do wit' yo' ass."

"Aw, okay. I assumed that because you brought me down to this concert you were feeling like it was my fault or something. I mean, I am sorry for having you bring me here because I would have been cool spending time with you anywhere."

Phoenix started the Porsche and punched the accelerator a few times igniting the pipes. They roared loudly. He closed his door and headed out of the parking lot. "Shawty you all good, that shit ain't yo fault by a long shot. Shit happens, everybody know that Memphis is the chain snatching, dope boy robbing, murder capital of the world. It been like that for a few years now. I just got caught lacking. That shit won't happen no more though." He started Durk and Lil Baby's, *Voice of The Heroes,* album nodding his head to the *Hats Off* track. "You had a good time though?"

Cassie nodded. "Yeah, I thank that's the most fun I done had in a long time. Kinda hope dis won't ruin you from coming to scoop me up from time to time. Sho' does suck tho."

"It's part of the game, shawty. I ain't gon' let that stop me from doing nothing. I done bought chains from some of the lil' young niggaz in Memphis before on some hot shit, so what goes around comes around. I ain't fucked up about it."

Cassie placed her hand on his knee. "So, you thank we can still enjoy these last few days that we got together, you know, just try an forget all about what just happened and what not?"

"N'all I ain't gon' forget, but I can most definitely try my best to enjoy you while I got you." He glazed all over her thick thighs and felt a stirring in his piece. Now that somebody had stolen three million from him, he had every bit of taxing Cassie's pussy on his mind. It would be the only thing that would keep him cool for the moment.

"Well, if it's all the same to you, I'd like to stay in for the next couple of days. We don't need to go anywhere unless you want to, but I'm easy breezy."

"That sounds good to me, lil' mama. We gon' see what's to it though." He swerved in and out of traffic and pulled up a halt at the stop lights twenty blocks away from FedX Forum. He eyed Cassie's thighs again in the Prada number that she wore. Her legs were tantalizing. He placed his hand on the left one and squeezed it. "What the hell yo' mama be feeding yo lil ass over there that got you running around all thick like this?"

Cassie giggled, "just food, whenever she does cook. Why what's wrong wit' how thick I am, you thank I'm fat or somethin'? Look, I ain't got no stomach'?" She raised her shirt all the way up to the underside of her braless titties, a hint of the areolas flashed Phoenix.

Before Phoenix could open his mouth to respond, two black vans slammed on their brakes in front of his Porsche and the side doors opened. He reached under the seat and grabbed his Glock .40. "Get down!" The masked shooters surrounded his car and proceeded to open fire rapidly.

Ghost

Chapter 18

"Yeah mane, I don't know why mafuckas be thanking fair exchange ain't robbery. Dis nigga, Lil Duke, gotta be out of his rabid ass mind to come from a family full of women and thank when he pulls some shit like he just pulled against yo' peoples that these slut hoez ain't gon' get slid on. When are niggaz gon' learn slime?" Three-O lowered the binoculars and placed them on his lap.

Pooh leaned forward and snorted two lines of heroin off a small mirror. He leaned his head back afterwards to allow for the drug to drip down his throat. "All I know is that were about to go in here and rape and kill every one of these bitchez. I'm talking from eight-eighty, my nigga. I wanna make this nigga pay. I done already popped a few Viagra so I'm good to go. I'ma sho' dis nigga Lil Duke what it is when you fuck wit' Choppa Gang. How many hoez you say in thurr right now?"

Three-O had the binoculars back over his eyes. "I see both of his thick ass teenage sisters, they mama fine ass, and one of her girlfriends. That's four bitchez in all. You tryna make all of them pay for his sins?"

"You muthafuckin' right I am. Dat nigga the one that brought family into this, not me. I been knowing where his people laid they head at. I drive past this mafucka every now and again and ain't once have I thought anything about harming dem folks. Now that he brought my family into dis hurr doe, it's open season, shawty and I been eyeing them sisters of his for a long time. It's about to go down, you can bet the house on dat." Pooh grabbed the binoculars from Three-O and peered at the four females that walked around Lil Duke's mother's home scantily clad. He licked his lips. "Hell yeah, I'm on dat."

"Well, you already know I'm fuckin' witchu the shiesty way. Let me pull dis trap 'round back and we are about to party these bitchez and make a statement. I guarantee you after tonight mafuckas gon' know what it is when you cross the gang, that's on every thang. Blurrrr!"

"Blurrrr Slime." Pooh returned.

***

Crash!

Natalia felt her back go inside of the China cabinet before it fell over loudly sending all sorts of glass and wood over the living room. She fell to her knees and groaned in pain. "You punk bitch."

Jahliyah stood up bouncing up and down on her toes. "Shawty, I was born and raised in Orange Mound. I've been fighting all my life. The system raised me; I don't know why the fuck you thought it was sweet wit' me."

Natalia rose and threw up her guards. She closed in on Jahliyah with her chin tucked. Jahliyah rushed her. Natalia jumped in the air and kicked Jahliyah in the stomach. Jahliyah stumbled backward and doubled over. She dropped to her knees in serious pain.

Natalia saw the opening and jumped on her back wrapping her arm around Jahliyah's neck falling to the carpet with her. "I told you I was gonna kill you bitch, didn't I? I always keep my word." She squeezed as hard as she could with her face balled up.

Taurus stood from the couch, though he'd promised the girls he would let the both of them fight it out and he wouldn't intervene, he was having second thoughts. He began to panic because of the choking sounds Jahliyah made. "Natalia, that's enough."

"Daddy, stay out of this, you promised." Natalia returned. She wrapped her legs around Jahliyah's back and pulled upward. She could feel her sister getting weaker and weaker by the moment. She was sure that at any second Jahliyah would go limp and then she could snap her neck. There would no longer be any competition. Taurus would be forced to love her and only her. A sick grin splayed across her face.

Jahliyah slapped her arms. She tried to reach around to pry her hold use but there was no use. It was impossible. She dropped her arms and became dizzy. Her eyes crossed. She could feel her heart pounding in her chest.

"Natalia, let her go! You're killing her." Taurus hollered.

"Stay out of it, Daddy! You promised!" She flexed her legs and heard a popping. She became giddy. She leaned forward and fell back hard, twisting as far left as she could. More pops sounded. Jahliyah went slack.

Taurus had seen enough. He ran over and tried to free Jahliyah. He hacked at Natalia's arms, but this only seemed to entice her to tighten her grip. Finally, after exhausting all remedies Taurus punched Natalia in the back of the head knocking her clean out. She fell forward. He pushed her to the side and grabbed Jahliyah. She was unmoving. He began to panic. "Jahliyah! Jahliyah! Baby, please wake up!" He laid her on the ground, slapping her cheek. "Wake up, baby."

Natalia rolled over holding the back of her head. She scooted backward with her face scrunched. She saw the scene between Taurus and Jahliyah playing out before her. It made her angry. She got up and ran toward the living room ready to grab her .9 millimeter from under the couch.

In her mind, Taurus had chosen who he loved the most and it wasn't her. She was over it, both of them had to pay the ultimate price. She could no longer take the emotional pain. When he got into the living room, she stopped in her tracks and almost had a heart attack as one man after the next dressed in all-black fatigues flooded into the living room heavily armed. Before she could make her retreat, she had so many red beams from their weapons all over her all she could do was raise her hands in surrender. She cursed under her breath.

Rondo slipped behind Taurus and slammed his shotgun to the back of his head knocking him to the floor. Taurus fell on top of Jahliyah. When he attempted to get up, Rondo cocked his automatic shotgun. "I wouldn't do that if I was you, Boss. That would be the worst mistake of your life."

Taurus turned over and mugged him. He could feel the stream of blood running down his neck. "Nigga, what the fuck you want wit' me?"

Rondo glared at him for a long time. "Everythang, and it's about to get ugly until I get it all, bitch. It's Shiesty Season and a brand-new day for the Duffle Bag Cartel.

To Be Continued...
Duffle Bag Cartel 7
Coming Soon

Submission Guideline

Submit the first three chapters of your completed manuscript to ldpsubmissions@gmail.com, subject line: Your book's title. The manuscript must be in a .doc file and sent as an attachment. Document should be in Times New Roman, double spaced and in size 12 font. Also, provide your synopsis and full contact information. If sending multiple submissions, they must each be in a separate email.

Have a story but no way to send it electronically? You can still submit to LDP/Ca$h Presents. Send in the first three chapters, written or typed, of your completed manuscript to:

LDP: Submissions Dept
Po Box 944
Stockbridge, Ga 30281

DO NOT send original manuscript. Must be a duplicate.

Provide your synopsis and a cover letter containing your full contact information.

Thanks for considering LDP and Ca$h Presents.

BAE BELONGS TO ME III

A DOPE BOY'S QUEEN III

By **Aryanna**

COKE KINGS V

KING OF THE TRAP III

By **T.J. Edwards**

GORILLAZ IN THE BAY V

3X KRAZY III

De'Kari

THE STREETS ARE CALLING II

Duquie Wilson

KINGPIN KILLAZ IV

STREET KINGS III

PAID IN BLOOD III

CARTEL KILLAZ IV

DOPE GODS III

Hood Rich

SINS OF A HUSTLA II

ASAD

KINGZ OF THE GAME VI

Playa Ray

SLAUGHTER GANG IV

RUTHLESS HEART IV

By Willie Slaughter

FUK SHYT II

By Blakk Diamond

TRAP QUEEN

RICH $AVAGE II

By Troublesome

YAYO V

GHOST MOB II

Stilloan Robinson

CREAM III

By Yolanda Moore

SON OF A DOPE FIEND III

HEAVEN GOT A GHETTO II

By Renta

FOREVER GANGSTA II

GLOCKS ON SATIN SHEETS III

By Adrian Dulan

LOYALTY AIN'T PROMISED III

By Keith Williams

THE PRICE YOU PAY FOR LOVE III

By Destiny Skai

I'M NOTHING WITHOUT HIS LOVE II

SINS OF A THUG II

TO THE THUG I LOVED BEFORE II

By Monet Dragun

LIFE OF A SAVAGE IV

MURDA SEASON IV

GANGLAND CARTEL IV

CHI'RAQ GANGSTAS IV

KILLERS ON ELM STREET IV

JACK BOYZ N DA BRONX III

A DOPEBOY'S DREAM II

By **Romell Tukes**

QUIET MONEY IV

EXTENDED CLIP III

THUG LIFE IV

By **Trai'Quan**

THE STREETS MADE ME III

By **Larry D. Wright**

IF YOU CROSS ME ONCE II

ANGEL III

By **Anthony Fields**

FRIEND OR FOE III

By **Mimi**

SAVAGE STORMS III

By **Meesha**

THE STREETS WILL NEVER CLOSE II

By K'ajji

IN THE ARM OF HIS BOSS

By Jamila

HARD AND RUTHLESS III

MOB TOWN 251 II

By Von Diesel

LEVELS TO THIS SHYT II

By Ah'Million

MOB TIES III

By SayNoMore

THE LAST OF THE OGS III

Tranay Adams

FOR THE LOVE OF A BOSS II

By C. D. Blue

MOBBED UP II

By King Rio

BRED IN THE GAME II

By S. Allen

KILLA KOUNTY II

By Khufu

<u>Available Now</u>

RESTRAINING ORDER **I & II**

By **CA$H & Coffee**

LOVE KNOWS NO BOUNDARIES **I II & III**

By **Coffee**

RAISED AS A GOON I, II, III & IV

BRED BY THE SLUMS I, II, III

BLAST FOR ME I & II

ROTTEN TO THE CORE I II III

A BRONX TALE I, II, III

DUFFLE BAG CARTEL I II III IV V VI

HEARTLESS GOON I II III IV V

A SAVAGE DOPEBOY I II

DRUG LORDS I II III

CUTTHROAT MAFIA I II

By **Ghost**

LAY IT DOWN **I & II**

LAST OF A DYING BREED I II

BLOOD STAINS OF A SHOTTA I & II III

By **Jamaica**

LOYAL TO THE GAME I II III

LIFE OF SIN I, II III

By **TJ & Jelissa**

BLOODY COMMAS I & II

SKI MASK CARTEL I II & III

KING OF NEW YORK I II,III IV V

RISE TO POWER I II III

COKE KINGS I II III IV

BORN HEARTLESS I II III IV

KING OF THE TRAP I II

By **T.J. Edwards**

IF LOVING HIM IS WRONG…I & II

LOVE ME EVEN WHEN IT HURTS I II III

By **Jelissa**

WHEN THE STREETS CLAP BACK I & II III

THE HEART OF A SAVAGE I II III

By **Jibril Williams**

A DISTINGUISHED THUG STOLE MY HEART I II & III

LOVE SHOULDN'T HURT I II III IV

Ghost

RENEGADE BOYS I II III IV
PAID IN KARMA I II III
SAVAGE STORMS I II
AN UNFORESEEN LOVE
By **Meesha**
A GANGSTER'S CODE I &, II III
A GANGSTER'S SYN I II III
THE SAVAGE LIFE I II III
CHAINED TO THE STREETS I II III
BLOOD ON THE MONEY I II III
By J-Blunt
PUSH IT TO THE LIMIT
By **Bre' Hayes**
BLOOD OF A BOSS **I, II, III, IV, V**
SHADOWS OF THE GAME
TRAP BASTARD
By **Askari**
THE STREETS BLEED MURDER **I, II & III**
THE HEART OF A GANGSTA I II& III
By **Jerry Jackson**
CUM FOR ME I II III IV V VI VII
An **LDP Erotica Collaboration**
BRIDE OF A HUSTLA **I II & II**
THE FETTI GIRLS **I, II& III**
CORRUPTED BY A GANGSTA I, II III, IV
BLINDED BY HIS LOVE
THE PRICE YOU PAY FOR LOVE I II

DOPE GIRL MAGIC I II III

By **Destiny Skai**

WHEN A GOOD GIRL GOES BAD

By **Adrienne**

THE COST OF LOYALTY I II III

By Kweli

A GANGSTER'S REVENGE **I II III & IV**

THE BOSS MAN'S DAUGHTERS I II III IV V

A SAVAGE LOVE **I & II**

BAE BELONGS TO ME I II

A HUSTLER'S DECEIT I, II, III

WHAT BAD BITCHES DO I, II, III

SOUL OF A MONSTER I II III

KILL ZONE

A DOPE BOY'S QUEEN I II

By **Aryanna**

A KINGPIN'S AMBITON

A KINGPIN'S AMBITION **II**

I MURDER FOR THE DOUGH

By **Ambitious**

TRUE SAVAGE I II III IV V VI VII

DOPE BOY MAGIC I, II, III

MIDNIGHT CARTEL I II III

CITY OF KINGZ I II

By **Chris Green**

A DOPEBOY'S PRAYER

By **Eddie "Wolf" Lee**

Ghost

THE KING CARTEL **I, II & III**
By **Frank Gresham**
THESE NIGGAS AIN'T LOYAL **I, II & III**
By **Nikki Tee**
GANGSTA SHYT **I II &III**
By **CATO**
THE ULTIMATE BETRAYAL
By **Phoenix**
BOSS'N UP **I , II & III**
By **Royal Nicole**
I LOVE YOU TO DEATH
By Destiny J
I RIDE FOR MY HITTA
I STILL RIDE FOR MY HITTA
By **Misty Holt**
LOVE & CHASIN' PAPER
By **Qay Crockett**
TO DIE IN VAIN
SINS OF A HUSTLA
By **ASAD**
BROOKLYN HUSTLAZ
By **Boogsy Morina**
BROOKLYN ON LOCK I & II
By **Sonovia**
GANGSTA CITY
By **Teddy Duke**
A DRUG KING AND HIS DIAMOND I & II III

A DOPEMAN'S RICHES

HER MAN, MINE'S TOO I, II

CASH MONEY HO'S

THE WIFEY I USED TO BE I II

By Nicole Goosby

TRAPHOUSE KING **I II & III**

KINGPIN KILLAZ I II III

STREET KINGS I II

PAID IN BLOOD **I II**

CARTEL KILLAZ I II III

DOPE GODS I II

By **Hood Rich**

LIPSTICK KILLAH **I, II, III**

CRIME OF PASSION I II & III

FRIEND OR FOE I II

By **Mimi**

STEADY MOBBN' **I, II, III**

THE STREETS STAINED MY SOUL I II

By **Marcellus Allen**

WHO SHOT YA **I, II, III**

SON OF A DOPE FIEND I II

HEAVEN GOT A GHETTO

Renta

GORILLAZ IN THE BAY **I II III IV**

TEARS OF A GANGSTA I II

3X KRAZY I II

DE'KARI

TRIGGADALE I II III

Elijah R. Freeman

GOD BLESS THE TRAPPERS I, II, III

THESE SCANDALOUS STREETS I, II, III

FEAR MY GANGSTA I, II, III IV, V

THESE STREETS DON'T LOVE NOBODY I, II

BURY ME A G I, II, III, IV, V

A GANGSTA'S EMPIRE I, II, III, IV

THE DOPEMAN'S BODYGAURD I II

THE REALEST KILLAZ I II III

THE LAST OF THE OGS I II

Tranay Adams

THE STREETS ARE CALLING

Duquie Wilson

MARRIED TO A BOSS… I II III

By Destiny Skai & Chris Green

KINGZ OF THE GAME I II III IV V

Playa Ray

SLAUGHTER GANG I II III

RUTHLESS HEART I II III

By Willie Slaughter

FUK SHYT

By Blakk Diamond

DON'T F#CK WITH MY HEART I II

By Linnea

ADDICTED TO THE DRAMA I II III

IN THE ARM OF HIS BOSS II

By Jamila

YAYO I II III IV

A SHOOTER'S AMBITION I II

BRED IN THE GAME

By S. Allen

TRAP GOD I II III

RICH $AVAGE

By Troublesome

FOREVER GANGSTA

GLOCKS ON SATIN SHEETS I II

By Adrian Dulan

TOE TAGZ I II III

LEVELS TO THIS SHYT

By Ah'Million

KINGPIN DREAMS I II III

By Paper Boi Rari

CONFESSIONS OF A GANGSTA I II III

By Nicholas Lock

I'M NOTHING WITHOUT HIS LOVE

SINS OF A THUG

TO THE THUG I LOVED BEFORE

By Monet Dragun

CAUGHT UP IN THE LIFE I II III

By Robert Baptiste

NEW TO THE GAME I II III

MONEY, MURDER & MEMORIES I II III

By **Malik D. Rice**

LIFE OF A SAVAGE I II III

A GANGSTA'S QUR'AN I II III

MURDA SEASON I II III

GANGLAND CARTEL I II III

CHI'RAQ GANGSTAS I II III

KILLERS ON ELM STREET I II III

JACK BOYZ N DA BRONX I II

A DOPEBOY'S DREAM

By **Romell Tukes**

LOYALTY AIN'T PROMISED I II

By Keith Williams

QUIET MONEY I II III

THUG LIFE I II III

EXTENDED CLIP I II

By **Trai'Quan**

THE STREETS MADE ME I II

By **Larry D. Wright**

THE ULTIMATE SACRIFICE I, II, III, IV, V, VI

KHADIFI

IF YOU CROSS ME ONCE

ANGEL I II

IN THE BLINK OF AN EYE

By **Anthony Fields**

THE LIFE OF A HOOD STAR

By Ca$h & Rashia Wilson

THE STREETS WILL NEVER CLOSE

By K'ajji

CREAM I II

By Yolanda Moore

NIGHTMARES OF A HUSTLA I II III

By King Dream

CONCRETE KILLA I II

By Kingpen

HARD AND RUTHLESS I II

MOB TOWN 251

By Von Diesel

GHOST MOB II

Stilloan Robinson

MOB TIES I II

By SayNoMore

BODYMORE MURDERLAND I II III

By Delmont Player

FOR THE LOVE OF A BOSS

By C. D. Blue

MOBBED UP

By King Rio

KILLA KOUNTY

By Khufu

<u>BOOKS BY LDP'S CEO, CA$H</u>

<u>TRUST IN NO MAN</u>
<u>TRUST IN NO MAN 2</u>
<u>TRUST IN NO MAN 3</u>
<u>BONDED BY BLOOD</u>
<u>SHORTY GOT A THUG</u>
<u>THUGS CRY</u>
<u>THUGS CRY 2</u>
<u>THUGS CRY 3</u>
<u>TRUST NO BITCH</u>
<u>TRUST NO BITCH 2</u>
<u>TRUST NO BITCH 3</u>
<u>TIL MY CASKET DROPS</u>
<u>RESTRAINING ORDER</u>
<u>RESTRAINING ORDER 2</u>
<u>IN LOVE WITH A CONVICT</u>
<u>LIFE OF A HOOD STAR</u>

Duffle Bag Cartel 6

Printed in the USA
CPSIA information can be obtained
at www.ICGtesting.com
LVHW020409120424
777133LV00037B/928

9 781955 270359